MYSTERY OF THE DRAGON'S GATE
DRAGONS OF ROMANIA
BOOK 6

DAN PEELER
&
CHARLIE ROSE

LUMEA PRESS
DALLAS TEXAS 2024

Dragons of Romania
Book 6

MYSTERY OF THE
DRAGON'S GATE

DW Peeler　　　Charles Rose

LUMEA PRESS

Mystery of the Dragon's Gate
Dragons of Romania - Book 6

First Printed Edition
1 3 5 7 9 10 8 6 4 2

ISBN 978-0-9856748-6-1 (Trade paper)
ISBN 979-8-9895936-1-3 (Hard bound)
ISBN 978-0-9856748-5-4 (ePUB)
ISBN: 979-8-9895936-2-0 (Audio)

Cover design by Charles C. Rose
Illustrated by Daniel W. Peeler

Published by
Lumea Press

This book is dedicated to

Judy Tucker

For over 40 years, with her sense of color, design, and sharp wit, she was our source for inspiration and whose love for the world around her extends out, like Dragons, far beyond the limits of the imagination.

Contents

1-The Vanished Leader

T anarul was happy to see his friend, Ayo, again. Several months had passed since their trip to Antarctica, and Ayo returned to his home in Africa. The two young Dragons had experienced quite a few adventures together, and seeing Ayo now gave Tanarul the feeling that another one was about to begin.

With Ayo, two other Dragons had also been approaching Tanarul's cave. Lumea, the most ancient of Dragons and mentor to Tanarul, was moving much faster than usual. Flying above him was another good friend, Viorica, the Dragon physician. Both had serious expressions on their scaled and craggy faces.

Ayo, also a flyer, had picked up his speed to be the first to reach their destination. The entrance to his friend's cave was blocked by a tangle of vines to prevent curious humans from exploring it, but Ayo easily flew over them and through the opening. He softly tiptoed his way through the twisting passage to surprise his friend. However, Tanarul's acute Dragon senses detected Ayo's presence early enough to slither to the ceiling where he could jump on his visitor's back. The two were wrestling and laughing when Lumea made his entrance.

Lumea's serious expression cracked into a smile. "Sorry to intrude on your privacy, Tanarul. I see you remember your old companion, Ayo."

Tanarul and Ayo immediately stood at attention before the revered elder Dragon, who was amused by their formal respect. Behind him, the bat-winged Dragon, Viorica, had made her entrance. She was much taller than the others and had to incline her long neck when she entered the cave.

Tanarul was happy to see both of his old friends. "You must have a major adventure planned. Viorica is with you, too!"

Lumea responded, "If we've learned anything by now, adventures are never planned. They happen. We have come to ask you to take part in a search."

"Bogdan is missing," Viorica added.

Bogdan, whose cave headquarters was in a secret site in Romania, was the Leader of All Dragons and a good friend to everyone present.

"Missing?" asked Tanarul, "Dragons sometimes disappear for a hundred years, and we live so long that nobody notices."

"That is normally true," replied Lumea, "but this time it's different. Bogdan was on his way to an important meeting with Chen, the Chinese Dragon, and he never made it there. Bogdan never misses an appointment."

"All of the flyers have been searching his route to China," said Viorica. "That's why Ayo is here. We even contacted the Hai Riyo. They couldn't find him either."

The Hai Riyo were super-fast Japanese Bird Dragons. A flock of them could cover the whole world in a matter of a few hours.

"It must have been an important meeting with Chen," Tanarul commented. "Bogdan seldom leaves Romania."

"There can be no doubt of that, "replied Viorica, "but the message didn't come to us from Chen himself. The Hai Riyo told us Chen was missing, too! We don't know what the meeting was about."

"Let's go to China and find out!" declared Tanarul.

"That's why we're here," said Ayo.

"We anticipated your response and could use your special detective skills," Lumea added

Tanarul didn't consider himself special at all. He just paid attention to what was happening around him. He was sure his friends were getting caught up in the tales that Vladimir, the Storyteller, had been writing. Vlad had always made Tanarul the hero in all the Dragons' current adventures, but the humble young Dragon saw no reason to protest the compliment at this point.

"Well, I detect that we're spending too much time talking. Let the search begin!" declared Tanarul.

The four of them immediately turned and headed out for the Cave of the Dragons, Bogdan's home and their official meeting place.

As they exited through the thick bushes, Tanarul paused long enough to say, "It's too bad Urk can't join us. He's truly the wise one!"

"Urk is still hibernating?" asked Ayo.

"He must be," Viorica answered.

"Yes, no one has seen him since you and Tanarul left for South America," added Lumea as all four Dragons entered the thick forest.

What none of them had realized was that there was a fifth Dragon who had been listening to their entire conversation. That same morning, the Lesser Dragon, Urk, had awakened from hibernation, and his first thought was to fly to Tanarul's cave and surprise his old friend.

It had been Urk, however, who had a surprise.

He had traveled on several journeys with Tanarul and, being no bigger than a shrew, Urk had spent most of his time riding in Tanarul's ear. However, soon after his emergence from his hollow tree, Urk had discovered, to his horror, that he had grown several times his original size.

He had also learned that he had developed the ability to breathe fire, now an impossible skill in Lesser Dragons. Urk was not truly skilled in the art at all; however, burning a tree to the ground by mistake. Usually jovial and sarcastic, he was now completely confused and silent.

Hidden in the rocks where he had eavesdropped on the four Dragons' conversation, Urk had some decisions to make. "I wish I could join them," he thought, "but I can't let them see me out of control. I just coughed and set fire to that tree! I'm not myself anymore! I'm about eight times myself!"

Urk knew that the true fire-breathers, the Greater Dragons, sometimes evolved during long hibernations. They might even grow wings or, rarely, another head. He had never heard, however, that Lesser Dragons, the small ones, could also evolve and change during hibernation periods. Some never hibernated since the Lessers had shorter life spans than the Greaters. This had been Urk's first hibernation.

"This is so frustrating!" Urk shouted in his own mind. Again, he attempted his fire-breathing abilities. He missed the stick he was trying to ignite and exploded the rock beside it. "This can't be happening!" he yelled aloud in the echoing forest.

Then, Urk sat up straight. "...but it is. I've got to put all those thoughts of what cannot happen behind me and pay more attention to what IS happening!"

He took to the air. His flying ability had not changed. He had always had wings. They were simply a lot bigger now. He was determined to find some answers, but there were so many unanswered questions: Seeing if he could control the fire? Adjusting to his increased size? Being able to face his friends?

Now, Urk disappeared into another section of the Transylvania woods.

Later, back at Bogdan's Cave, the four Dragons had learned, to nobody's surprise, that there had been no further developments in the Mystery of the Vanished Leader. Lucian, the young Romanian human who often visited the cave, met them at the entrance. Years ago, he and his Ethiopian friend, Makeda, had formed the Human/Dragon Alliance. It consisted of a group of people who were levelheaded enough to grasp the fact that there were intelligent talking Dragons in the world. These humans also understood that Dragons were not village-burning monsters, but ancient and wise beings who were concerned about the future of our planet.

Lucian was with Vladimir, the Storyteller. The two of them spent a lot of time together. Lucian was always hungry for more stories about Dragon history and Vladimir was always pleased to find an eager audience for his tales.

"Tanarul!" shouted Lucian, "if you are on the search now, I'm sure Bogdan will be found in no time!"

Tanarul laughed and greeted the young human. He gave a side-glance to a grinning Vladimir. "Vlad's stories about me are giving me too much to live up to. Your knowledge of human tech has saved us more than his imaginary 'Great Tanarul' stuff."

"Well, Great Tanarul," said Vladimir, "Your imaginary skills are still needed in the Far East. As Lucian mentioned, our leader is still nowhere to be found."

"Which would mean Chen is still missing, too," said Lumea. "Lucian, have you established contact with your Chinese branch of the Human/Dragon Alliance?"

"Yes, Great Lumea," Lucian answered, respectfully as always, "and I let them know to expect the four of you soon. I knew Tanarul would be ready for another challenge!"

"Safe guess, Lucian. Tanarul lives for adventure," laughed Ayo.

Tanarul just shook his head.

"If you fellows are through exchanging compliments and witty remarks, I suggest we take Tanarul's latest adventure to the sky," said Viorica, already flapping her wings, "You're the strongest flyer, Ayo. You take the lead!"

The much-younger Ayo was surprised by the more-experienced Viorica's complement, but he did not hesitate to take to the air. "Let's go to China!"

Tanarul waved to his two friends and was airborne, too. He and Lumea were not winged Dragons. They could leap for great distances and soar for miles on wind currents. The breezes Ayo and Viorica always stirred up would carry them for many miles.

"I'm guessing that I'm invited as well," said Lumea, also sending a little wave as he, too, disappeared into the thick Romanian clouds.

Lucian turned to Vladimir. "I always get a major buzz when I see winged flyers like Ayo and Viorica take off, but I'm even more amazed to see Tanarul and Lumea take off without wings, just like superheroes!"

"It is quite a sight," Vladimir observed, "but there's more chemistry than comics in their abilities. They inflate their lungs with their own fire-breath. The heat doesn't make them lighter than air, but it greatly reduces their weight. They spread their cheek fins for balance. They're pretty superior jumpers, too!"

Lucian sighed, "I would love to write down all I've learned about Dragons, but so much has already been written. I'm sure whatever I would write has been said before by some other human."

Vladimir thought for a moment while the two of them still looked skyward. "I have had the advantage of watching human development for many years. They have a long history of talking a lot, and writing a lot, too. Yes, Lucian, what you might write down about our race has probably been said before. However, I have also noticed that humans have an even longer history of not listening."

Lucian sat up straight and intent, making sure Vladimir could see he was not one of those humans.

Vladimir continued, "It is very likely that most of them will think that whatever you have written is something brand new; amazing facts that they have read for the first time! That is how some writers become labeled as creative geniuses... by people who simply have not ever listened before."

"Ha!" Lucian replied, "or more likely, by people who have never read anything before!"

"Sadly, true," said Vladimir. "But if you were to write our history, you do have one great advantage! It would be written according to genuine, living Dragons' perspective. It would be the whole truth!"

"But people don't want to read about the truth," sighed Lucian. "Most think it's boring."

"Then, promote your stories as fantasy fiction!" laughed Vladimir, "and fool them into hearing the truth!

"Trick them into learning the truth?" Lucian was in deep thought.

"Young man," laughed Vladimir, coughing up a smoke ring, "Do you want to sell your stuff or not? Just write."

Urk had never been in such a dense section of the Transylvania Forest before. He discovered at his increased size. He could cover greater distances much faster. Most Lesser Dragons spent most of their lives near the regions where they hatched. When they traveled longer distances, they were usually in the company of Greater Dragons.

He had been to Australia several years before at the invitation of the Australian Dragon, Bert the Bunyip, who had given him a ride to his home. Staying long enough to learn Australian slang had helped Urk do a little translating for his newer friend, Tanarul, years later. After meeting Tanarul, Urk had become probably the most-traveled Lesser Dragon in history, but always as a passenger in his friend's ear.

"I've got to learn to watch my speed," thought Urk, "and this forgotten forest would be a good place to try it."

For the next few hours, he chose a few landmarks, such as a distant tree or a rock formation. He knew how long it would have taken him to reach his goal in the past. Now, he timed himself at his new size. On each trial, he calculated that he was at least eight times faster.

"I wonder how strong I am?" he suddenly thought.

Lesser Dragons are naturally strong, being able to pick up and carry objects several times their own weight. Urk remembered flying with a laptop once, carrying it for his human friend, Makeda, at the Cave of the Dragons. He had not given it much thought at the time.

Urk looked around for something to lift. He came across another pile of rocks of varying sizes. Starting with one of the smaller stones, which seemed to weigh nothing to him, Urk finally worked his way up to a large boulder. With a little bit of effort, he managed to lift it off the ground.

He carefully put the big rock back in place. Dragons, of course, took care to never make major changes in their environment. "Just as I figured! I'm also eight times stronger! Speed and strength seem pretty easy to control, but I'm still in need of some training to master my fire breath! Where can I find that out here?" he shouted aloud in frustration.

"Well, certainly not from any of us," said a soft voice that sounded like a gentle breeze blowing through a hollow log."

Urk flew to the top of the rock pile and was not surprised by what he saw on the other side. He could not imagine the sound of that melodic voice coming from any other being except a Padure Dragon. He also realized that Dragons are never alone, even when they are in a remote of forests.

The Padure Dragons appear almost identical to trees, with rough skin that looks like trunks and branches and large extended scales that could easily be a huge variety of leaves. There are millions of them standing in silent guard duty throughout every forest in the world.

"If you are looking for instructions in flame throwing, the Dragons of the forest will be of no help to you," continued the Padure, "since we are surrounded by kindling."

"I would never ask one of you to breathe fire!" exclaimed Urk, "since the kindling is also your kin. You couldn't risk igniting a niece or second cousin."

"You are most understanding, Young Dragon," the tree-like creature commented.

"I'm not that young; just small...but not nearly as small as I used to be...it's complicated to explain," Urk stammered.

"I have thousands of years to listen," smiled the Padure.

"Well, before I was this size, I was a very small Lesser Dragon. Then I hibernated. When I woke up, I had changed. Now, I've grown into a smaller Greater Dragon, I think... primarily because I have increased powers and can breathe fire! I'm not very good at it, though. In fact, I'm awful at it. Understand?" asked Urk.

"I understand that you have been very careful about breathing flames in the middle of the forest, and we appreciate that," said the Padure. "My sisters and brothers have been watching you practice for hours. We have decided that your needs can best be served by one of the Ancients who lives nearby."

Urk thought he had met just about every Greater Dragon of Romania. They had been making their appearances very often at the Cave of the Dragons in the last few years. "An Ancient One lives out here?"

The Padure nodded its leaf-covered head. "Yes, one of the originals. She has been in hibernation for a few thousand years. One of the Oak Padures spoke with her a few weeks ago. She related a story about going through a few hibernation changes, too. Her cave is near the Poodle Rock three hills away from here."

"The Poodle Rock?" asked Urk.

"I know," said the Padure, "rock formations should have more noble names like The Eagle's Claw or The Lunging Bear. This one just happens to look like a Poodle. What else can I say?"

"A landmark is a landmark, as far as I'm concerned," said Urk, "and as long as this one helps me get where I'm going, I don't care if it's called The Curly Pig Tail Rock."

"That one's on the other side of the river," the Padure casually commented, "but try Poodle Rock first. That's where the Great Balaur lives."

"Balaur?" exclaimed Urk, "The Balaur family used to be the most famous Dragons in all of Romania! As a matter of fact, the humans in Romania call all of us 'Balauri', which is the general name for all dragons."

"Yes, all of the original Balauri went into hibernation many centuries ago," replied the Padure. "This is the first of them we've known to walk the land since the days before the rat plague wiped out the humans in this region."

Urk didn't follow much of human history, but he presumed that must have been a very long time ago. Before the Padure had a chance to point out another rock formation called the Sickly Rat, he quickly thanked the helpful tree Dragon and took to the sky. It was time to meet the Great Balaur.

2-The Great Balaur

"The Padure was right. It does look like a Poodle," thought Urk as he passed over the third hill and the rock formation came into view. He landed on the top of one of the enormous boulders that named the formation. There was a curling pattern eroded in them that could pass for the tufts of fur that crown the heads of the elegant canines.

He jumped down to the jutting oblong rock that served as the dog's snout and looked below it for signs of the entrance to a cave. He knew that the Greater Dragons usually masked the openings with piles of rocks or fallen trees to protect their privacy. He had no idea how long it would take to find the cave.

After exploring for about an hour, Urk detected the sounds of an intense conversation happening nearby. He quickly realized that his increased size had not only enhanced his strength but also his hearing. He flew toward the muffled voices, which became more distinct as he discovered a small crack between the top two rocks of a pile that closed off the entrance. He squeezed his head through the crack and listened.

"Fire breath is a gift common to all of us," said the first voice, "but fire breathing is a skill that requires discipline."

"Yes," said the second voice, "a skill that separates a satisfying feast from a stack of charcoal."

"But won't my stomach be satisfied by the foods the two of you eat?" asked the third voice.

"That would be convenient, wouldn't it?" laughed the first voice, "except that we have three stomachs!"

"Each of us has a stomach?" said the third voice. "How unusual."

This statement had Urk needing clarification. "Of course, the three of them would have three stomachs," he thought. He had to maneuver through the rocks to view the voices' source. After some intense squeezing and even more careful lifting of the maze of rocks, he silently made his way to a partial view of the Dragons in question.

He could see their three heads resting their chins on three stalagmites that had eroded into large, rounded bumps throughout the centuries. As each of them spoke, she would raise her head slightly to look into the eyes of the other two. Their bodies were hidden behind the stalagmite wall, and Urk chuckled silently to himself, saying that they gave the appearance of a dragon puppet show with himself as their only audience.

However, he didn't find the show very entertaining since they were continuing the confusing conversation about their stomachs. As they chatted, Urk recognized them as Balaur Dragons since he had seen the pictures

Tanarul had drawn in one of his Dragon history files. They had cheek fins and long twisting horns that occasionally clicked with the Dragons' horns next to them as they turned their heads to speak. Finally, to Urk's relief, they stopped talking about their stomachs and resumed discussing how to breathe fire. The Dragons to the right and the left were instructing the Dragon in the middle.

"All animal life in this cave is quite healthy," said the Dragon on the right, "so we'll have to explore outside to find a dying creature destined to be our prey. You'll need a bit of practice to learn how to find just the right roasting temperature for your fire stream."

The Dragon on the left raised her arm and pointed her finned hand toward the rocks hiding Urk. "The top rock on that pile will be a good target. Let's try some intense heat first. Take a deep breath and see if you can melt it."

Urk froze. The Dragon was pointing directly to the rock he was crouched behind!

In the meantime, Lucian and Vladimir still discussed Lucian's Dragon history book project at the Cave of the Dragons.

"Lucian, much of your writing will have to be dedicated to 'un-telling' the false Dragon history that humans have been spreading for centuries," said Vladimir.

"I realize that," Lucian replied. "My nation's history is full of sensational fables about horrible monsters: Dragons who hoard gold and steal princesses while they take a break from burning down villages and forests."

"Oh yes, we are the ruthless villains that populate nightmares and bad movies; the images of evil!" shouted Vladimir, unfurling his bat-like wings and assuming a forbidding pose. In the process, his wing breeze jarred Lucian's morning teacup off its flat rock. It shattered on the rocky ground.

"Terribly sorry, old chum," said Vladimir softly as his wings slowly lowered to his sides. "I'll replace it, of course."

Lucian laughed. "At least it was just a teacup, not an entire burning village full of screaming children."

"Hmmm, uh, yes," said Vladimir, regaining his historian composure. "The humans of Europe, like most of their species, have generally seen us as creatures they dread more than any other. Another of their characteristics is to classify and label us just as they, unfortunately, classify and label each other. I wish I had some of Tanarul's sketches here to show you what I mean."

"I have all of them right here on this tablet," declared Lucian.

"Ah, your technology," smiled Vladimir, "a convenience that often escapes me. May we, what's the word...crawl through them?"

"Scroll through them," smiled Lucian. "I thought Dragons never forget."

"Dragons never forget things worth remembering," mused Vladimir as Lucian began to scroll. "There...That one. Can you un-scroll for a moment?"

Lucian had stopped on an image of Tanarul himself.

"Wingless Dragons, such as Lumea and Tanarul," said Vladimir, "are classified by some humans as Drakes, not as Dragons at all. They are seen as dragon-like with four legs, sort of relatives of real Dragons. Drakes can walk on all four legs or upright on only two, as our friends do. This is the first myth you need to address. Tanarul is undoubtedly 100% Dragon.

"The term for this second illustration comes closest to describing Dragons such as Viorica and me," Vladimir continued, "since we have webbed wings on our long fingers, much like a bat, and one set of legs. Some Europeans have historically called us Wyverns, which they still consider relatives of Dragons, a sub-species. We are Bat-winged Dragons. I will give you details later about what true Wyverns are.

Lucian continued to scroll down his selection of Tanarul's illustrations. "Pause on this one," requested Vladimir. "Most humans define this one as a worm. As you can see, she has a long, curling body, like a serpent, that tapers into a long tail. People also spell their species like a common earthworm is spelled. They are variations of Serpent Dragons. We'll talk more about her at length, too.

Lucian continued his scrolling. "And this would be the last one in their simplified definitions of us," said Vladimir, "with four legs and a massive set of wings growing out of the back, it's the only one the European Dragonologists label as a True Dragon. The other three are described as occasionally having the ability to breathe fire. Sometimes, non-fire-breathing Drakes have been known to have wings, but this one, the one they call a True Dragon, is always a fire-breather.

Lucian shook his head. "These labels seem wrong on so many levels. I've seen all of you breathe fire. The only Dragons that don't are the Lesser Dragons, and the Europeans seem not to know those."

"The humans don't know of the Lessers because that is how Dragons classify themselves," said Vladimir.

"And many Dragons," Lucian replied, "including Tanarul and Ayo, don't like that labeling system. 'Dragons are Dragons! Big or small! Fire or no fire!' I've heard Tanarul say that a lot."

"It is wise to listen to young Tanarul," said Vladimir. "He is a rule changer."

Lucian chuckled at hearing a two-hundred-year-old Dragon being described as "young."

At that very moment, Urk was not concerned about the differences between Greater and Lesser Dragons. All he knew for sure was that he was being confronted by not just one but three Great Balauri and the one in the middle was about to blast his rock hiding place with her volcanic fire breath. There was no time to fly away. All he could do was crouch down and hope her aim was terrible.

Her aim was alright. Her narrow, scorching stream of flames was immediate and precise, centered on her target rock behind which Urk was cowering. The rock glowed for a couple of seconds and then melted into a lava-like mass, covering the top of the rock pile and completely engulfing Urk himself.

"Death by molten rock," moaned Urk, "Liquidated!" Then, the thought struck him. "If I'm thinking, I must still be alive! And this molten rock; it's no warmer than a sunny summer day to me." He stood up straight and shook the searing lava off his body like a toppled bowl of oatmeal. "The ability to withstand extreme heat!" he thought. "Another Greater Dragon advantage."

"Oh dear, what have I done?" said the surprised middle Dragon.

"A visitor!" declared the one on the right.

"A very sturdy visitor!" said their friend on the left.

"I didn't plan on intruding on your private conversation," said Urk, "but the Padure told me you might be able to give me some directions on my flame-throwing." He then let out a big uncontrollable hiccup and belched a few smoke rings.

"I would have taken you to be an Urkind dragon, except for your size," commented the Dragon on the right. "Yet, you are a fire-breather. I've never known a Lesser Dragon to breathe fire."

"Neither have I," sighed Urk. "It's new to me, too!" The Padure said that there was a Balaur in this cave, one who might have an answer to my burning question. Now I see that there are three of you."

"Three of us?" said the center Dragon. "The Padure was correct. There is only one." They all rose in unison from their reclined position to their full height, spreading one set of broad wings behind them. Urk could now see that he was talking to a massive single Dragon who happened to have three heads.

"Now I wish I had been a better listener to Vladimir's stories," Urk commented, "because I'm sure some of his Balaur tales mentioned that you had a dozen or so heads."

"Vladimir?" asked the right head, "We've been in hibernation for about eight hundred years, so we haven't been keeping up with current events."

"...But it seems that some of those old stories are still making the rounds," said the left. "Most Balaur families have only one head, but three is the limit. It was a human exaggeration that multiplied our numbers."

"That makes me the last head in this trio," said the middle head.

"We are thrilled about her arrival, too," said the right head. "She joined us very recently, during our eight-hundred-year hibernation. Now we're a complete set."

"Why are three heads a complete set?" asked Urk.

"Shouldn't it be obvious?" said the left head. "Imagine having two heads, each one being an independent thinker. What if each head wants to fly in the opposite direction from the other one?"

"We used to have discussions and sometimes arguments for hours," said the right head, "and usually decided on going nowhere. Now, we have a third head, a tiebreaker. With two heads in agreement, the third will gladly follow the majority rule."

"That does make a lot of sense," said Urk, "but what if the third head wants to fly in a third direction?"

"Well, then we would…uhhh," stammered the left head. All three heads were silent momentarily, glancing at each other eagerly, waiting for a response.

Urk broke the silent pause by asking, "How long have you been a complete set?"

"Only about a couple of weeks," said the middle head, "since I joined the team sometime during hibernation and we awoke twelve days ago. Incredible things can happen to a Dragon during hibernation."

"Yes, I know!" lamented Urk. He then explained his story about recently waking up eight times his average size. "I adapt well to most changes, except for the fire breath. It's just all over the place."

"It's not an easy skill to master," said the left head. "That's why we are training our newest member."

"And since I just came close to barbequing you," said the middle head, "I think a favor is in order. Would you like to join me in the training sessions?"

"Being trained by one of Romania's most legendary Dragons?" thought Urk. "How could I say no?" he exclaimed out loud. "I came here for a little advice, and now I'm a student at Balaur U!"

"Balaur, You?" asked the middle head. "Do you mean Balaur, Us?"

"Not you," replied Urk, "I was saying 'U' –The letter 'U' which is short for University. Humans in this century like to abbreviate everything."

"I see. Well, we have been absent for eight hundred years," said the right head. "I have a good idea. We can learn a lot from you, too!

"In Human years, what century is this, Urk?" asked the left.

"The twenty-first," Urk replied.

"Hmmm, that would mean St. Francis of Assisi is no longer with us. I'll miss him." said the left head. "And the knights, those Slayers of Dragons; are they still roaming around?"

"The knights have been gone for many years," Urk answered.

"Well, that's a plus," said the right head. "I suppose things are pretty quiet in this 21st century."

"The human population of the earth has increased quite a lot in the last 800 years," replied Urk, "and I'm sure you can imagine that they are not what we would call quiet."

"Dear, dear, dear, those humans," said the left head, shaking back and forth. "I'm not anxious to hear about all the messes they've caused, not immediately, anyway."

True, true," said the right head. "Let's begin with a situation we can control. Girls, Light up your burners! It's time for Dragon-breath lesson, number one!"

3-The Mysterious East

Ayo's flying speed was faster than Tanarul had ever remembered, and Dragons have perfect memories. All four Dragons were anxious to arrive in China. Lumea had some old friends there - wise teachers. They might have a few answers about the disappearances of Bogdan and Chen. Even the winged Dragon, Viorica, benefited from the wind currents Ayo stirred up. Lumea and Tanarul had not been forced to land once to renew their souring leaps into the air.

Ayo was as concerned as the others about the disappearance of their leader, Bogdan, but he was also excited to be visiting China for the first time. Before meeting his new best friend, Tanarul, and the other Romanian Dragons, he had seldom flown more than the length of his own country.

Ayo's family preferred the privacy of their caves hidden deep within Africa's Mount Kilimanjaro. His knowledge of the more fantastic world of Dragons had been confined to the lessons he had learned from his wise teacher, Yakini. She had painted wonderful word pictures about the lives of their majestic relatives in the Far East. Finally, he was about to meet them.

An experienced world traveler, Viorica had been flying a short distance behind Ayo, navigating their journey. They were now approaching the city of Hong Kong. As always, the Dragons were invisible to humans as they glided above the highways and between the tall buildings. Chameleon-cloaking was a skill common to all of them.

"Over there," directed Viorica, "through that big opening in the bank building."

Ayo made a graceful dive as the others followed his lead: down, down. They passed through a massive portal from the sea view side of the bank to the mountain view of the building's back. They reduced their speed to glance right and left through the large windows at the many human residents busy with work. The people would have been amazed to see four Dragons in flight just outside their windows, but they did not see the spectacle.

In passing through the building, Tanarul noticed that other buildings besides the bank had similar openings at different levels. All faced the sea, with the mountains at the buildings' rear entrances.

Tanarul turned to Lumea, who was gliding beside him. "Why do so many of these buildings have these large openings in their middle?"

"An appropriate question," Lumea answered. "They are called Dragon's Gates. The people of China have great respect for their Dragons. Their legends tell them that the mountains are the Dragons' homes. When this modern generation started building their skyscrapers, the designers decided they should have openings and doorways through which the Dragons could travel.

Their stories tell them that the mountain-dwelling Dragons descend to refresh themselves in the sea every morning. The Dragons' Gates are their entrances to the waters."

Before Tanarul could ask his next question, Viorica quickly ascended above Ayo. "Our goal is the mountain peak where Bogdan and Chen were last seen."

The four of them were now settled in a small, grass-covered valley, no larger than a soccer field, except it was more of an oval shape. Walls of jagged rocks surrounded the flat green area. Graceful trees with small leaves grew here and there among the rocks. Tanarul immediately recognized the location. He and Lumea had enjoyed a quiet afternoon's conversation with the Chinese Dragon, Chen, at that place several years ago. The young Dragon wished to return soon and hear more stories. Now, he was finally back, but Chen was nowhere to be seen. His large cave was dark and empty.

Tanarul turned to Ayo. "This is where I learned the secret of the wingless Chinese Dragon's ability to sky-swim; you know, flight without wings."

"Oh, yes," said Ayo, "Your inflatable scale story! I wish I could hear Chen himself tell it."

"If we are successful in our quest, you will," said Lumea.

"What information do we hope to gather in this empty field?" asked Viorica.

"Maybe some news from a friend," Lumea answered.

In unison, the four Dragons suddenly looked skyward. Their sensitive Dragon- -hearing had detected the faint flapping of leather wings from a distance away. Against the sun, they could now see the silhouette of a graceful flying creature.

"Wings!" Ayo exclaimed. "That can't be a typical Chinese Dragon."

"Oh, there are a great variety of Dragons in this ancient land," said Lumea, "and not all of them are sky-swimmers."

As the visitors grew near, they could now see what Lumea meant. This flyer did have leather wings and what appeared to be a long flowing mane along the back of his arched neck. He was bright yellow, with glistening scales and a Dragon tail covered in generous amounts of long flowing hair. As he touched down beside them, they saw that his body shape appeared more like a horse than a Dragon.

"Longma!" exclaimed Lumea, "Please allow me to introduce you to my friends."

Tanarul was familiar with the stories about China's Dragon Horse, the messenger of the nation's community of Dragons. Longma, or Huanglong, as some humans called him, was also known as the Dragon of the Earth. The ancient Chinese people divided the essential elements into five: Earth, Water, Fire, Wood, and Metal. Each of the components had a Dragon as its symbol.

"Lumea," exclaimed the Yellow Dragon, "When I was told you would be visiting China, I was most honored to learn you would be visiting me! And now I see that the Great Tanarul is among your companions!"

Tanarul was instantly embarrassed. Vladimir's colorful stories about the bold adventures of the young Dragon had reached China.

Lumea found Tanarul's humility refreshing but also a little amusing. "Yes, indeed," he answered, "and joining the Great Tanarul are his faithful assistants, Viorica and Ayo."

Tanarul was shaking his head at his teacher's latest attempt at humor, but he and the others politely greeted the kind and very impressive Longma.

"Along with my joy about your visit, I did feel an equal amount of dismay, however, considering the reason for your trip here," said the Dragon Horse. "We have continued the search for our missing friends while we awaited your arrival, but without luck, I'm afraid."

"Are the Dragons of the Directions joining in the search?" asked Viorica.

"Yes, and all four will be joining us soon. I saw them as I flew this way." Longma replied.

Since their earliest days, the Chinese Dragons have been exceptionally well organized and coordinated in their duties. They were specific about their assigned territories to protect. The Dragon of the North China Sea, folding his spine wings as he landed, was called Heilong, the Bringer of Winter and Water. He was black and glistening.

The Dragon of the South, a sleek Dragon with no back fins, was named Chilong, the Red Dragon from the South China Sea. Chilong was the bringer of Summer and was called the Great Dragon of Fire.

The Dragon of the East, Qilong, with a winding snake-like body and lion's mane, was a striking blue-green color and the bringer of the welcome season of Spring. Qilong also was designated as the Dragon of Wood and lived in the East China Sea.

The last Directional Dragon, the bringer of the Autumn season, came to them from the West and wound his long body to the point that it was difficult to decide whether he was arriving or leaving. Bailong, the Dragon of Metal, could become glowing white at will and lived in Lake Qinghai.

Chen's cave was enclosed by a double door fashioned from two gigantic triangular rocks that only a dragon could swing open. Longma escorted the Dragons into the depths of the cave, where each of them looked for clues.

"It would help a lot if we knew what we were looking for," said Ayo, "since all we know at this point is that they have disappeared. I doubt they left a note."

"Bogdan is a great leader and very considerate," said Viorica. "Dragons don't usually leave notes. He likely would have taken the time to contact a local Dragon with his departure plans. That's just who he is."

"Yes, Bogdan would have done that if he and Chen had left willingly," said Tanarul.

Lumea was the last to enter the cave. He had been silent throughout most of the conversation. "I believe it is safe to presume that they did not."

Urk's flame-throwing control had gradually improved. He wasn't nearly as awful as he had been at the beginning. He was grading himself in the 'half-awful' category now. Meanwhile, he had gotten to know his teachers better. He had learned that Carra, Laura, and Raluca were the three personalities.

Urk updated the three-in-one Balaur about current Dragon history throughout their fire-breath training lessons. He also told them some of the highlights of the past 800 years of human history. Since humans had never really interested him, highlights were all he could offer.

Carra, whose head had been the series's original, knew the most about human/dragon relations. She was surprised to learn that the Romanians now called all Dragons the Balauri since she knew so many other species did not resemble her family.

"Humans have a talent for confusing things that had once been very clear," she commented. "I supposed we should be flattered that they have labeled all Dragons as Balauri. Someone in our family must have done something special to deserve that."

"Or maybe the humans had never met any other Dragons," said Urk.

"That's more likely," said Laura. "We're simple and ordinary country folks."

"Yeah, with three heads," said Urk. "That usually leaves an impression on humans."

"How many heads do humans usually have?" asked Raluca.

"Only one," Urk answered.

"They must get very lonely," Raluca concluded.

Urk chuckled, being a mono-headed creature himself. He suddenly stopped to think about what Raluca was saying. He was in the Balaur cave to learn to control his new abilities to enjoy reuniting with Tanarul, Ayo, and his other companions. Without them, he was beginning to feel lonely. He had missed their last adventure because of his need to hibernate. His first thought was to surprise Tanarul when he awakened, but his transformation prevented that reunion.

"Lonely?" said Urk. "I never thought much about that, Raluca. I've spent most of my life surrounded by the other Lesser Dragons in the fields or hanging around the mouth of the Cave of the Dragons. There is so much activity there! This is the first time I have thought about what it's like to be lonely."

"Dragons need each other just as humans need each other," said Carra. "Since you are not fortunate enough to have at least one other head to keep you company, I suggest we redouble our efforts to prepare you for an overdue visit with your old friends!"

Urk's enthusiasm immediately returned. "The three of you are one great friend. I'll be a good student to surprise Tanarul with the brand-new Urk-Plus! Complete with fire breath to die for!"

"To die for?" asked Laura.

"It's just another 20th-century thing that humans say," Urk explained. "Like most of their expressions, it's not literal. It means something like the best thing ever."

The three heads tittered with uncomfortable laughs as Urk's mind wandered one more time to thoughts of Tanarul and the others. "Hmmm, I'm sure the four took to the sky days ago. They must be in China by now."

The Dragons of the north, south, east, and west had already begun to join the Dragon Horse and his four Romanian guests.

Their entrance was as dramatic and spectacular as should be expected of four legendary creatures emerging from behind the steep surrounding cliffs. Slowly floating skyward, traveling precisely from each of the four directions, they quickly darted toward a point in the clouds over the center of the field. The four of them looked as if they were about to collide, but they slowed down as quickly as they had sped up. Joining clawed hands and forming a circle, the four Dragons began slowly circling and descending simultaneously.

Back in the African plains, Ayo had witnessed human skydivers floating downward in this sort of formation. The humans depended on the opening of their parachutes to ensure a safe landing. One of the four Dragons had the advantage of wings to help the others do the same job.

Tanarul seemed to be taking particular notice of the wings. Lumea answered his question before it was asked. "These four are the most ancient of all the Dragons in this part of the world. They have known many hibernations. The appearance of wings has completed the evolution of one. The others will likely sprout them, too.

As the black, white, red, and blue-green Dragons came closer, Viorica observed, "What a show. I'll bet it's their routine ceremony whenever they appear in the same area."

"Correct," said the Yellow Dragon Horse as he trotted to the center of the field. He froze in position and became the center of the compass the descending Dragons had made. On landing, each Dragon had his tail pointed in the exact direction of his origin.

No one had to ask which Dragon was which. Their bright colors told their story. "We have a theory, Great Western Friends!" announced the glistening White Dragon.

"We have read about each of you in Vladimir's books, so no introductions are necessary," added the Dragon of the East, "And I am certain you know who we are."

"Our friends are still nowhere to be found," said the Black Dragon of the North.

"But, we have a good idea of where that 'Nowhere' is," concluded the Red Dragon of the South.

"Do the Chinese Dragons speak in riddles, too?" Tanarul whispered to Lumea.

"Most certainly," Lumea replied, "but they answer their riddles immediately."

"'Nowhere' is the other side of the Gate!" exclaimed The Black Dragon.

"That's an answer?" Ayo whispered to Tanarul.

"You're saying that the Dragon's Gate has re-appeared?" asked Lumea.

"That is our theory," said the Blue-Green Dragon, "You are the only one among us who is honored to be able to remember all the times it has appeared."

"Yes, I am certainly old enough to remember," said Lumea, "but I was occupied on the other side of the globe the first time I heard of that event happening. It was in the early years of the first Ice Age. I heard other stories about it throughout my history. The last time was about ten thousand years ago."

"Didn't we just pass through a Dragon's Gate on the way here?" asked Tanarul.

"The humans of this culture have built structures with that same name wherever they have settled throughout the world," said Lumea. "They pay tribute to us with their Dragon's Gates, but none of them is aware of the existence of a real one."

"And this gate leads to 'Nowhere'?" asked Ayo.

"That is our awkward attempt to define something without definition," explained the Black Dragon. "Our history tells us of a passage, a portal that cuts through the atmosphere. No Dragon can resist passing through it. From our perspective, it disappears as quickly as it opens, leaving the Dragon nowhere."

"Is it a gate, a rectangular shape like the Dragon's Gate we passed through in Hong Kong?" asked Tanarul.

"To our knowledge," the Red Dragon replied, "the real Dragon's Gate is more of a round opening. This is the teaching of our ancient ancestors."

"Round?" asked Tanarul. "Do you know if it just fades into view or if it opens and closes from the center like a camera lens?"

"Our ancestors made no mention of this camera attachment of which you speak, Great Tanarul," said the Blue Green Dragon. "The ancients would not have known your knowledge of the world of humans and their devices. We have told you all they have told us."

"What is our next step?" asked Viorica. "Do we patiently wait at the cave for another ten thousand years until the Dragon's Gate opens again?"

"Oh, it could happen anywhere at any time," said the Dragon Horse, "not just in this location. I have heard stories of the Gate appearing in several Islands people call the East Indies and as far away as Hawaii."

"Australia and New Zealand as well," added the White Dragon.

"Do you suppose there are Dragons in those places who can tell us more about it?" asked Tanarul.

"There are!" replied the White Dragon. "We can direct you there."

"They are the Dragons of the directions, after all," whispered Ayo in Tanarul's ear.

Tanarul smiled and suddenly had pleasant flashbacks about some of Urk's sarcastic comments inside his ear, even though it had been a while. He missed Urk's quick wit.

"The first Dragon who might be of some help would be the Taniwha of New Zealand." said the White Dragon. "She has some first-hand information about the Gate."

"A trip to the islands of Hawaii could also be useful," said the Blue Green Dragon. "You could talk to the Dragon Goddess, Kihawahine, about her experience."

"I can direct you to the Mindi of Australia, where another Dragon's Gate story is told," added the Red Dragon.

"There are also Dragons north of here who have such stories," said the Black Dragon of the North. "One is none other than Druk of Tibet, the Protector of Shangri-La."

"It sounds as if this trip has just begun. Where do we go first?" asked Ayo, "Hawaii or Shangri-La?"

4-Dragons of Maui

It was a quiet evening at the Cave of the Dragons, more peaceful than Lucian could remember since he had first started his regular visits there. His first Dragon friend, Cosmina, who had found Lucian unconscious in the nearby woods, was home in her cave that evening. She had been so kind to him and had nursed him back to health until his injuries from his hiking fall had healed entirely. Tonight, his thoughts were filled with images of Cosmina and the many other noble Dragons he had met and befriended since that time.

Vladimir and the other regular cave visitors had left as well. The cave seemed so vast and empty now, mainly because of the absence of Bogdan. This was not just the headquarters of the Human/Dragon Alliance; it was Bogdan's home. Lucian wondered if Tanarul, Ayo, and the others had made any progress in the search for their missing leader.

He also missed his friend Makeda, the Ethiopian girl who had helped establish the Human/Dragon Alliance. She was still in Africa visiting her great-grandmother, who was very ill. Her last text let Lucian know that the end was near for her ailing Nana. He sent her the usual words of comfort that humans exchange at such times, but he knew that Makeda realized that words were never enough to explain the emotions that are felt when death parts us. Lucian felt so small and powerless in the vast Dragon cave.

The emptiness of the cave made the fantastic evening seem to grow even colder, and Lucian felt the need to build a little campfire to relieve the chill and serve as a reminder of his near-immortal fire-breathing friends. After stacking the branches and sticks and being ready to light the fire, he suddenly remembered he had no matches. There was no need for them at a cave usually full of creatures that could light campfires with a sneeze. Lucian stared at the stack of timber and felt more deserted than ever.

"Hey, Bruh, need a light?" said a voice out of the darkness behind him. Before Lucian could turn around to see who had joined him, a stream of fire shot over his shoulder, and the pile of sticks was already blazing.

Lucian stood up and looked in all directions behind him, but no Dragon could be seen. "Hello? Where are you? Thank you for the fire, but who are you?"

"An old friend," said the voice, again behind him, but this time hovering over the fire.

Lucian whirled around and finally saw the tiny Dragon that had warmed his life. The visitor looked familiar, but something was not right about him. "When I first glanced at you, I thought you looked like my friend, Urk, but you're about ten times his size."

"about eight times. Thanks for the compliment," said the visitor.

Lucian was shocked. "Urk? Are you Urk? What happened? And, hey, you're breathing fire. I didn't know you could do that."

"You're thinking of the old Urk, the pre-hibernation model," he said, "Observe!"

The little Dragon dived down, picked up a boulder over three times his size, and quickly flew it to a position on the other side of the campfire. He settled down on it. "There. Now I have a place to sit for our chat."

"Do Lesser Dragons always proliferate?" asked Lucian.

"I seem to be the first one," said Urk, "and it's terrific to see you, Lucian."

Lucian was still in disbelief. "You seem also to have grown in another way, Urk. Before, all I got from you was a joke or two and a quick buzz around my head. It's terrific to see you, too!"

"I'm glad I can talk to you before I see the others," said Urk, "I'm not myself anymore. I can't begin to think about fitting into Tanarul's ear at this size. He'll be disappointed."

"Oh, Urk," laughed Lucian softly, "we humans worry about things like fitting in! You're a Dragon, the world's coolest creature! It would be best if you didn't have any worries at all. And Tanarul- he must be the kindest, most understanding Dragon in the world!"

"Sometimes you're pretty smart, Lucian," said Urk, "almost Dragon-like! Oh, I hope I'm not insulting you."

"An apology?" said Lucian. "You are still amazing me. You just paid me the highest compliment I can imagine."

"May I tell you something else?" asked Urk.

"Anything," Lucian replied.

Urk paused for a moment. "I'm lonely for my friends."

"I'm sure you are, Urk," said Lucian, "and I know they're missing you, too. Just before they took off for China, Tanarul said it was too bad you were still hibernating."

"They miss me?!" said Urk. "I need to go there! I can control my fire now, and they could use my help!"

"You couldn't control your fire before?" asked Lucian.

"Not at first," Urk replied, "but a good friend with three heads taught me quite a few tricks of the flame."

Any other human might have been startled at the mention of a friend with three heads, but Lucian had once had a conversation with the nine-headed Hydra. He just nodded and said, "A triple-good friend."

"Can you help me, Lucian? Can you find out where they are?" Urk asked eagerly.

Lucian quickly grabbed his phone. "I have some friends who can."

As was their custom, the Romanian Dragon search-and-rescue party had broken into two teams. Lumea and Viorica were headed to New Zealand to meet with Taniwha, the contact mentioned by the White Dragon. Tanarul and Ayo were about to arrive at the Hawaiian Island of Maui. The Blue-Green Dragon had told them of a location where they could learn the whereabouts of Kihawahine, who also had some critical information about a Dragon's Gate.

Since their mission was urgent, Tanarul had hitched a ride, holding onto Ayo's tail. There was no time to ride the wind currents. "In the Hawaiian Islands, Dragons are called 'Mo'o,'" said Tanarul. "Their language is lovely here. Lumea has taught me a few phrases. Look! That has to be the labyrinth the Blue-Green Dragon told us about."

Labyrinths look like giant mazes drawn on the ground by humans. They are a circular winding path but not designed to trick the walker with dead ends like a maze. They have one path that leads both into the center and out again to help the visitors focus their thoughts while walking. This pathway was beside the beach, and the strong surf washed through the weathered rocks beneath the rugged shore. It was called the Dragon's Teeth Labyrinth because of the jutting rock formations beside it. The path was often covered with tourists, but at the time, the Dragons were the only two visitors to the beach.

On landing beside the grassy rock-lined path, they noticed extreme winds. The labyrinth itself had a little shrine in its center covered in stacked photographs of people and religious objects, along with what seemed to be some found beach items, such as old flip-flops. Nearby some black lava sand beaches had very dangerous blowholes which could suck careless people into the ocean below and drag them out to sea.

"We should return here one day and walk this labyrinth when we have more time," said Tanarul. "These pathways were designed by the most peaceful of humans, people who care about blending their hearts and minds with the spirit of the planet."

"People like Lucian and Makeda?" asked Ayo. "They take care of the earth just like Dragons!"

"Yes! People like them!" said Tanarul.

They were interrupted when the sound of a solid geyser-like spray of ocean water shot up from one of the shoreline blowholes. A second blast revealed the dark shape of some creature enveloped in the mighty stream. As the water was sucked back down within the pounding surf, Ayo and Tanarul could see clearly that the beast was a powerful-looking Dragon standing upright with his arms crossed, like the genie of a magic lamp.

"Honored visitors, allow me to introduce myself. They call me Kapulei, Mo'o of the Labyrinth," declared the Dragon in a booming voice.

Ayo struck a similar impressive pose. "They call me Ayo, Dragon of uh...the Wind! This is my friend Tanarul, the cleverest Dragon in all of Romania!"

"Don't tell me," declared Kapulei in an even more booming voice, "Qilong, the Blue Green Dragon of the East, sent you! And you have come seeking audience with the Goddess Kihawahine!"

"How did you know this, wise Kapulei?" asked Tanarul.

Kapulei's voice dropped. "Oh, because no one ever comes to see me. They always want to see her. Also, most visiting Dragons are usually sent here by Qilong. It was an excellent chance you were, too."

"I have no doubt that you have many wonderful stories to share as well, Kapulei," said Tanarul, "but we have been sent here on Dragon's Gate business."

"Oh, if that is the case, Kihawahine is the Island expert!" said Kapulei. "I'll fly you there myself."

"We are indebted to you, Great Dragon of the Labyrinth," Ayo said, "and by the way, that was the most spectacular entrance I've ever seen."

Kapulei raised his head and shot out a massive stream of vertical fire, then admitted, "It's even better when I end it with a burst of flames. I choked a little on some water just now. Next time, it will be even better, I promise."

"We'll tell all our friends," said Tanarul.

"Off to the pool of Lahaina!" said Kapulei. "It's the Goddess' home. The three of them were quickly airborne. Ayo and Tanarul were glad to have the personal tour. There was a lot of dense jungle ahead, and the pool was well hidden.

"The pool is just beyond that Banyan Tree," said the Labyrinth Mo'o. They thanked him as he gave them a dramatic bow, saying farewells before returning to his seaside home. Taking to the air, he called back, "Don't bother diving into the pool to find her. She'll find you."

He had been correct about diving into the water not being necessary. The moment they landed on its far shore, they could see a long and graceful shape spiraling to the surface. Kihawahine's very regal-looking face quickly emerged from the water as she spoke.

"I sensed the presence of two Mo'o from the other side of the globe the moment you arrived at the Labyrinth," she said. "Aloha awakea."

"Aloha awakea to you as well, Great Island Goddess!"

Kihawahine turned to Ayo. "We are saying 'good noontime', Ayo."

Ayo was shocked. "You know my name? You must be a Goddess."

"I know exactly who both of you are, brave and gallant Ayo, but I'm more a good reader than a Goddess. Your companion is the Great Tanarul. I have read about your adventures in those charming tales your Romanian friend Vladimir has been spreading all over the Dragon world."

"You're correct about our names, and I must admit that Ayo is the bravest Dragon I've ever known," Tanarul replied, "but Vladimir always flatters me too much. He calls me 'Great' as his little inside joke. He knows I think titles are silly, Goddess Kihawahine."

"I see," Kihawahine replied. "You are saying the title 'Goddess' is also silly?"

Tanarul was immediately flustered. "Oh, no! I didn't say that at all! You are the greatest legendary Mo'o in the Islands. I'm sure you deserve that title! And the respect that comes with it! I'm saying that I do not deserve to be called 'great' because I've done nothing to earn that label!"

Kihawahine smiled her glistening tooth-filled Dragon smile. "Hmmm...it seems you are certainly 'great' at explaining yourself, and flattery is one of your skills, too. Well played!"

"I hope you can forgive my insult to your high station," said Tanarul. "I would never..."

Kihawahine tried to keep from laughing but couldn't. "I'll forgive you if you show me what a good detective you are. Vladimir always mentions the quality of your character in his stories. He can't be wrong about everything. You came here looking for information about the Dragon's Gate. See if you can find it in this story."

"He'll find it!" declared Ayo. "Tanarul rules!"

"Ah, always his champion," Kihawahine noted. "Vladimir was right about that, too, I see. Now, on to the story:

"The people of these islands made my name famous in several stories. One is an old tale about my tricking one of their heroes, Chief Puna, into marrying me. The story is not even close to the truth, which makes it very similar to your European Dragon Legends. The appearance of the Dragon's Gate within the tale is completely accurate, however."

Both Ayo and Tanarul settled down to listen intently.

"The tale begins with Chief Puna seeking a wife among the Island Goddesses. He runs across two of us, a Goddess named Haumea and me. He falls in love with

Haumea and asks her to marry him, not knowing I have already fallen in love with him. He does not realize that Haumea and I are shape-shifting Dragons disguised as beautiful Goddesses.

"After the marriage, the story continues to say that I became so angry and jealous that I ran away to feel sorry for myself on some remote island. A few days later, Puna gets an urge to go surfing and somehow appears on the beach of that island. I convinced him that the waters there were not suitable for surfing, leading him to an even more remote and unchartered desert area. This one is so far away that he cannot find his way home, and I keep him there as a prisoner in my cave.

"Many trickeries, escape plans, chases, and discoveries follow this. During this time, Puna is horrified to discover that I am a Dragon and finally makes his way to the edge of the crater of Mount Pele. By now, I have recruited a pack of angry Dragons to help me find and kill Puna. For some reason, the Volcano Goddess, Pele, has taken pity on Puna, and the volcano suddenly erupts, spewing lava all over the other dragons and me.

"I take flight and escape, but three other Dragons do not. The lava is so hot that they are gone in a flash as a fourth dragon leaps out of the way. Puna escapes me forever. More adventures follow, and I finally flee to Maui, where I have dwelt in a deep pool near Lahaina to this day."

"Wow, that's quite a story," said Ayo, "and we know that at least part of it is true since you live in Maui and this pool near Lahaina."

"As to the rest of it, I'm sure it's fiction," said Tanarul, "the part that is hardest to believe is that your Dragon companions were so easily destroyed by the lava erupting from Mount Pele. Every Dragon knows that volcano fire does not affect us. Even if they did disappear in a flash, it wasn't from the heat. They were vanishing into a Dragon's Gate!"

Kihawahine broke into loud laughter that caused a few waves in her pool. "Vladimir was correct about your detective skills, young Tanarul. The part about the Dragons on the edge of the volcano is true. Certainly, we were not there to chase any human. The five of us were avoiding being stoned by a group of them while we were out for a stroll. They were chasing us just for being Dragons. When three of our party decided to fly away, they flew directly into the Gate...and zap! They were nowhere! The humans made up the rest of the story after they witnessed the blinding flash."

"You did see that happen?" asked Ayo.

"As Tanarul correctly concluded," said the Dragon Goddess, "That was a real Dragon's Gate event."

"Can you tell us exactly how the Dragon's Gate appeared?" asked Tanarul.

"That is one of the most interesting parts of the story," said the Dragon Goddess. "At first, I saw a point of light.

As it began to spiral outward, the sky in its path seemed to change from blue to a color I can't describe. Based on what I saw, 'Hollow' is the best term. The point of light had now become a bright glow that outlined the hollow circle.

The three flying Mo'o picked up their speed and headed directly toward its middle. They seemed anxious to enter it. They disappeared into this hole in the sky, and as quickly as it had been formed, the point of light spun in a reverse spiral back to the middle; three streaks of lightning shot out as it closed, and the Gate was wiped away."

"Sort of like the opening and closing of a camera lens you were talking about, Tanarul," Ayo said to his friend.

"It seems to be, except without the lightning," Tanarul answered.

"An odd thing about the lightning was that it was not followed by thunder," mused Kihawahine.

"Hmm, no thunder," said Tanarul.

"And the lightning never struck the ground," the Dragon goddess continued. "It just streaked over the horizon and out of sight."

"Very strange," said Tanarul. "Can you tell us if the point of light opening the Gate spun clockwise or counterclockwise?"

"Clockwise," she answered, demonstrating the photographic memory shared by all Dragons.

"Why is that detail important?" asked Ayo.

"I'm not certain it is, but at this point, all details are important," Tanarul answered.

"Any news yet?" asked Urk.

"I've texted Bertie the Bunyip in Australia," Lucian answered. "He's that incredible bulldog-faced Dragon with the Internet in his cave."

"Yes, yes, I know Bertie. I've been there, you know," said Urk, "What did he say?"

"He said he would contact Human/Dragon Alliance friends in China for me," said Lucian, smiling. "I don't speak Chinese, you know."

"Sorry to be so anxious," said Urk. "A China flight is a pretty long distance for me."

Lucian was now reading the latest text from Bertie. "Hmm, a Hawaiian flight is an even longer distance. That's where Bertie says Ayo and Tanarul are now."

"Hawaii?" exclaimed Urk, "Looks like I've missed another adventure."

Lucian scrolled through his messages again. "It seems Bertie has also arranged a ride for…"

Before Lucian could say "you," a Hai Riyo, one of the super-quick Bird Dragons of Japan, had appeared on a rock beside them.

"Please allow me to apologize in advance," said the Hai Riyo. "We are unsure if they are still on the Island of Maui or have already left. Also, carrying you as a passenger will slow me down. It could take me up to eleven minutes to find them."

"I'll take along a magazine to read," said Urk, hopping onto the Hai Rio's back. "Lucian, I want you to know how grateful I am f........."

The Hai Riyo and his passenger had disappeared.

"Let's see," said Lucian to himself, glancing at the clock on his phone, "They must be over India by now."

5-Report from New Zealand

Viorica and Lumea had followed the lead of Bailong, the White Dragon of the West. They were both familiar with the Taniwha of New Zealand. Bailong was not sure about the exact location of the huge Dragon since Taniwha are tunneling creatures. They live in a maze of tunnels deep beneath the beautiful country's jungles, hills, and swamps. Lumea, however, had a friend in the islands. He was sure he could get advice on the Taniwha's current home.

Viorica, the mighty winged Dragon, flew in the lead as Lumea rode her wind currents.

"Let's make a quick stop in Tasmania," said Lumea. "That's where my old friend lives. He knows everything that's happening on the islands."

Tasmania is an island below the east coast of Australia and directly west of the island chain of New Zealand. As the Dragons sailed over the remote area, they could see two Tasmanian Devils on a grassy plain near the coast. "They seem to be arguing," said Viorica.

"Oh, that's just how Tasmanian Devils talk to each other," said Lumea. "They yell a lot."

The two Dragons landed softly on the grass near the two animals. The two creatures paid no attention to the Dragons but continued their yelling match. "I don't speak Devil," said Viorica. "What are they yelling about?"

"Food," Lumea answered. "It's always about food. Where the food is, how much food is there, who else might want their food. It is a necessary conversation but not very interesting."

The two Dragons waited for a break in the discussion. Finally, one of them breathed, and Lumea asked in perfect Tasmanian Devil dialect. "I'm sorry to interrupt such a fascinating conversation, but can either of you tell me where the Kurreah might be today?"

"Kurreah?" yelled one of them. "The Boobera Lagoon, I imagine. He's usually there."

"Do you know where in the lagoon?" asked Lumea.

"This time of day, he wouldn't be in it," yelled the other. "He'd be hanging beside it."

"Sunning himself!" yelled the first one. "Hanging in a tree. He's got a prehensile tail. They're good for that."

"Yes, yes, I know," said Lumea, "and we are most grateful for your help."

"G'day, mate!" the two Tasmanian Devils yelled together. Then, they quickly returned to the vital business of yelling about food.

"He's near a lagoon not far from here," Lumea said to Viorica, "and such a short distance, I can hop there. Follow me."

The two Dragons reached their destination, Boobera Lagoon, in less than five minutes. They were in a remote, well-hidden part of the island, far from civilization. This had been true of their entire trip so far. They had not once been forced to use their chameleon camouflage to mask their presence from humans.

"The Tasmanian Devils said, or rather, yelled, that he would be hanging from a tree, sunning himself," said Viorica. "Let's try that grove over there."

The trees were thick near the bank of the lagoon, but soon, they spotted some bright patches of orange among the greenery.

The Kurreah was indeed hanging upside down from a very sturdy limb. His long tail was coiled around it, monkey-style. On closer inspection, they could see that he had bright orange stripes around his entire lengthy body and patches of red, blue, and a very bright green, much lighter than the trees. His neck was decorated with long frills like many Australian lizards.

The stunning Dragon immediately sensed the presence of two more of his kind. He slowly began to bend in the middle and raise his head. As the frills started falling from his face, Viorica could finally see Kurreah's head and very long snout.

She had heard of him. Immediately, she understood why humans often mistook him for an enormous crocodile if his head was all they could see sticking out of the water.

He uncoiled his long tail and somersaulted to the ground. A small leaf-covered branch broke off the limb and landed on his nose. He sneezed a small stream of fire and smoke. He was a Dragon.

"Lumea!" said the Kurreah, breaking into a crocodile smile, "Are you back in Australia for a visit with Bertie?"

"Not this time, Kurt," Lumea replied. "We have come looking for directions."

"Surely the Great Lumea is not lost!" laughed the Kurreah. "But, please excuse my rudeness for not welcoming your friend to Boobera!"

Viorica introduced herself and apologized for disturbing his rest. She quickly outlined their mission. "We are not lost, but our Leader, Bogdan, is -or missing, I should say. Several of us have flown to this part of the world from Romania to look for some clues that could help us find him. We suspect there is some Dragon's Gate involvement."

"The mysterious Dragon's Gate!" said the Kurreah. "I have heard many old stories about its appearances but no new ones for many years. However, I can tell you who has the Taniwha of New Zealand."

"That is the exact reason for our visit, Kurt," said Lumea. "Bailong of China tells us she has had some personal contact with the Gate, but we have no idea where in New Zealand she might be."

"I should be able to figure that out," said Kurt. "The Taniwha you need to see is named Karutahi. I call her Kari. The Maori People highly revere her. I remember, back in the human year 2002, the government of New Zealand was about to build an expressway over the swamp where Kari lives.

The Māori culture protested to the point that the expressway plans were altered. I'm sure she still lives where she is so respected."

"The Maori are a very wise people," said Lumea. "They don't fear Dragons. They revere Dragons."

"They are very grateful for the wonders of the planet we share," said Kurt. "In 2012, they organized another protest. This time, it was about a proposed tunnel under Auckland that would have cut through the tunnels of another Taniwha's home."

"What name have the humans given the expressway that avoids the Taniwha Kari's swamp?" asked Viorica.

"The swamp is off to the side in the middle of the road, between their cities of Hamilton and Auckland. It is named for them," said Kurt.

"We must fly to the Hamilton-Auckland Swamp!" declared Lumea. "We are indebted to you, Kurt."

"I hope Kari can help you find Bogdan," said Kurt, "but go there remembering what my mother once told me."

Viorica and Lumea had already taken to the sky. She looked over her shoulder and asked, "What did she tell you?"

Kurt called back to her, "Beware the Dragon's Gate!"

Lucian was no longer alone at the Cave of the Dragons. Two Padure Dragons had emerged from the forest to resume their regular guard duties at the cave's mouth. Even though Bogdan was still missing, his loyal tree-like guards had faith in his return. Vladimir was also returning, flapping his enormous bat-like wings into their landing position. Following him through the low clouds was his friend Phoebe, the leader of the Phoenix flock.

"I see you are wasting no time writing your Dragon book," said Vladimir.

Lucian casually looked skyward from his tablet. He was used to being blown sideways by approaching winged Dragons.

"It's about time I started writing down what I know about your world. I'm loving it. Even before I met Cosmina in the deep forest, I was interested in Cryptozoology," said Lucian enthusiastically.

"Cryptozoology?" asked Vladimir.

"Cryptozoology is all about searching for animals most people think are myths or are thought to be extinct," said Lucian.

"Animals like the fantastic mythical Phoenix?" laughed Phoebe.

"Exactly," Lucian answered, "The Phoenix, the Loch Ness Monster, Bigfoot, and the Yeti are favorites of those stories, especially Nessie. I've heard so much about her from Tanarul."

Lucian scrolled his collection of WEB articles about Cryptozoology. "The explorers constantly post articles about their dead-end Loch Ness expeditions. Look at this one, Vladimir. It's dated September 9, 2019. The headline says, 'No Monster DNA in Loch Ness.'

It says, 'After years of painstaking research, this group of respected scientists has determined that there is no trace of DNA of either dinosaur or modern lizard in Scotland's famous body of water.' We both know that Nessie and her family have lived in Loch Ness for centuries. I would think that this DNA search would have revealed some evidence."

"But there is a major flaw in the premise of their research, Lucian," Vladimir replied. "They are looking for evidence of dinosaurs or giant lizards. Dragons are neither of those. Nessie is a Dragon. Since no Dragon DNA has ever been discovered, they couldn't possibly recognize it."

"That makes perfect sense," said Lucian, "Too bad they're wasting so much time looking for the wrong monster! I could tell them that what they are trying to locate is not a monster, but their main goal is to prove there is no Nessie."

"Some humans waste a lot of time trying to prove wonderful things are not real," sighed Phoebe.

Lucian agreed with the Phoenix and was about to make another observation when he glanced at his phone. It was barking.

"Bertie?" asked Vladimir.

"Yes, it's Bertie," Lucian answered, a bit embarrassed.

"I'm sure Bertie would be very flattered by the barking ringtone," said Vladimir, "Bunyips take pride in their resemblance to bulldogs. What's Bertie's news?"

Lucian checked the message. "He says that Lumea and Viorica are still following clues given to them by the Black, Red, White, and Blue Green Dragons of China."

"Ah...yes, the Dragons of the Four Directions," commented Vladimir. "I'm sure they sent Tanarul and Ayo to Maui as well. Where are the other two headed?"

"Bertie says, "to New Zealand and Shangri-La," Lucian replied. "Hey, is Shangri-La real?"

"It's as real as the Loch Ness Monster," said Phoebe.

"Wow...and look at this," said Lucian. "Bertie's source of information is the Chinese Dragon Horse. I've never read about a Dragon Horse."

"Longma, the Dragon Horse!" exclaimed Vladimir. "If you intend to write your book, it would not be complete without the messenger and guardian of the earth.

"I've heard many Dragon Horse stories from my Phoenix friends in China," said Phoebe. "The Chinese legends say that he was born of an ordinary mare after she drank from a stream where a Dragon had been bathing."

"Is that true?" asked Lucian.

"It makes a good story," said Vladimir. "In reality, even Dragons are unsure of the origins of many of our species' members. We are a diverse family. I know that Longma has a horse-like neigh that sounds like the haunting music of a flute."

"Yes, and I'm told that he brought the diagram people now call the yin-yang to Emperor Mu of Jin," said Phoebe.

"I hope Tanarul brings back a drawing of Longma!" said Lucian.

"No doubt he will. I hope you can meet the Dragon Horse himself one day, Lucian," said Vladimir. "He can explain the I-Ching to you, too. Another story gives him credit for rising out of the Yellow River to present that divination system to the same Emperor."

"I-Ching, the Book of Changes!" squawked Phoebe, "Chinese cosmology!"

"I can't wait to add this story to my book!" exclaimed Lucian.

"Excellent. Never wait to write your story!" said Vladimir, "Ideas are fickle and fleeting!"

Viorica had flown over the beautiful islands of New Zealand many times, marveling at the great forests and mountain ranges. It seemed odd to her to be back there again. This time, she was chameleon-cloaked against the clouds and following the path of an expressway.

"As long as the humans are confined to traveling in those wheeled vehicles, the whole world will be embroidered with those winding strips of concrete," sighed Lumea, sailing once again on the winged Dragon's air currents.

"Don't complain too much," said Viorica. "I prefer having humans safely on the ground rather than facing billions of them up in the air with me."

Viorica stopped chatting suddenly, jarred higher into the clouds by some unseen force. Lumea began to spin behind her as the air current she had created was immediately broken. He floundered toward the ground. Viorica quickly recovered her wing control and dived in Lumea's direction. She grabbed his hand and flung him skyward, where he regained his gliding balance. Viorica resumed her place in the lead, flapping her wings even faster and providing solid currents for the elder Dragon to ride.

"What just happened?" yelled Lumea. "Was that an air pocket?"

"Not an air pocket," Viorica answered, "I know how that feels. It was some barometric pressure disturbance. I can't identify it yet."

"Neither of us has ever been near a Dragon's Gate," observed Lumea. "Could it have been another one about to open?"

"I hope not. All we know about the Dragon's Gate at this point is that it somehow takes Dragons into it," said Viorica. "I would like to have a lot more information than that before we get near one."

"Up ahead!" exclaimed Lumea, "The city of Auckland. The expressway that connects to Hamilton is in that direction." As he extended his arm to point, Lumea again lost his balance and fell again.

"You are a Dragon of many skills, but I've had much more flying time than you have. Grab my tail for balance," said Viorica. "I'm anxious to feel the ground under my feet again."

Lumea was happy about the lift. They quickly flew together over the large city, where they spotted the expressway to Hamilton. After a few more minutes, they were nearing their goal.

Breaking into a glide, Viorica exclaimed," Look over there. That must be the swamp Kurt described. I'm not anxious to get my wings wet, but we should begin our search."

"I don't believe that will be necessary, my friend," said Lumea. "The Taniwha has come to us."

A Dragon's chameleon-cloaking ability never fails to work when walking unseen among humans. It is not that simple for Dragons if they wish to hide from each other. Lumea, who counted his years in the millions, had an advanced ability to detect the faint outline of another cloaked Dragon immediately.

"Yes!" said Viorica. "Now I can see her, too. Flying may not be your number one skill, but I'm always amazed by your keen vision." Lumea let go of Viorica's tail so that he could flip into landing mode.

"I believe that would be Kari herself, lounging on that steep rock bank," Lumea noted as he tilted into a descent. He inhaled an extra amount of his fire breath, inflating his lungs to make himself lighter for a soft landing.

Kari was not used to visitors. Long ago, she and the rest of her Taniwha kin had decided that tunneling and living under swamps, hillsides, and cities was preferable to making public appearances. She loved the Maori People and was flattered by their worship of her, but she resolved never to take credit for the magic those humans had assigned her. She did enjoy an occasional chameleon-cloaked visit to the surface, where she could admire the natural beauty of the swamp that had been preserved for her pleasure.

Lumea had spotted her instantly. Her lengthy body was nestled in the crannies of the rocky shore. Utterly invisible to humans, her features became even more focused on the two Dragons. Her appearance was striking. Except for her long and sharp row of spines running the length of her back, Kari strongly resembled the tuatara lizard, unique to New Zealand.

The Taniwha slowly raised her head. "Visiting relations from Europe?"

Lumea politely bowed. "Romania, to be exact, Great Karutahi."

"I'm afraid you are too late to help on White Island. The volcano erupted much quicker than we expected."

"A volcano! Of course!" exclaimed Viorica. "That was what caused that barometric disturbance! Where is White Island?"

"Too far off the southern coast for us to reach now," said the Taniwha. "Even Hai Riyo's speed would be of no use now. The damage is done."

"Were there human inhabitants on the island?" asked Lumea.

"I understand there were some," said Kari, "but none live there. The only humans would have been tourists."

"Sadly, humans do not have the instincts we animals do," lamented Lumea, "There is no doubt the wildlife on White Island sensed the coming disaster hours before the eruption and fled to safety."

"I remember when humans had much sharper instincts than now," said Kari. "The people who call the Taniwha magic have forgotten that they used to be magic, too."

"Magic happens when we relax into doing what is natural to us!" declared Viorica. "I'm always having that discussion with some human friends back in Romania."

The Taniwha looked confused. "If you didn't come here on your way to the volcano, what brings you to our beautiful island?"

"The Dragon's Gate," stated Viorica.

Kari sat straight on her haunches with her long tail curled tightly around her whole body. She began to tremble and seemed to be in shock. "You came through a Dragon's Gate? How is that possible?"

"No, we didn't come through a Dragon's Gate," said Lumea. "We came here hoping you could give us some information about them."

Kari began to relax. Her tail started to uncurl slowly. "That's a story I regret, I can tell. Who sent you? Was it Kurt or one of the Dragons of China?"

"Both!" said Viorica and Lumea together.

"Sounds important," Kari observed, "but what's the emergency? It has been thousands of years since a Dragon's Gate appeared; before, these islands had no highways, roads, or even trails."

"We believe one appeared in China just a few days ago," said Viorica.

"But you didn't see it?" asked Kari. "Did anyone else?"

"Bogdan, the Leader of the Dragons and our good friend, is thought to have disappeared into a Dragon's Gate," said Lumea.

"Chen, the Great Dragon of China, apparently went with him," added Viorica.

"No one saw it happen," said Lumea," but all four of the directional Dragons, as well as the Dragon Horse, are sure it was a Dragon's Gate that caused their disappearance."

"I cannot question the wisdom of those five," said Kari, "but I don't have much hope for your friends. No Dragon has ever escaped from a Dragon's Gate. I witnessed several members of my own family vanish through one many years ago, and they have not been seen since."

"We are so sorry to hear that!" said Viorica. "Can you describe what happened?"

"Sadly, yes," said Kari. "Three of my younger brothers and I were swimming in the ocean to the west of here. They proposed a race to the great island the humans now call Australia. I agreed but decided to hold back a short distance to let the young ones win. They were looking back at me, laughing, and making arching dives like our dolphin friends, when up ahead of them, I could see a long strip of the water beginning to boil. I stopped swimming and called for them to return, but their laughter kept them from hearing my warnings. Then I saw it appear."

"The Dragon's Gate?" asked an excited Viorica.

"That's the name I learned later from the Dragons of China," Kari answered. "It was huge and round, like a great disk, and as it rose from the waters, I didn't understand what I was seeing. All around its circumference was a hot, brightly glowing strip of light. It looked like the entrance to an enormous tube or cave with a cloudy void beyond it, but none of the sea was being sucked inside. Finally, it cleared the waters, and I could see it was perfectly round.

My brothers had swum closer to it by now. Before they could turn their heads around to see what I was yelling about, all three of them immediately began floating in mid-air. Then, they were gone. They had tumbled through the Dragon's Gate in less than a second. A point of brighter light began to trace a path around the glowing edge, decreasing the size of the Gate with each rotation. In another two seconds, the point had reached the center; some streaks of lightning without thunder shot out over the horizon as it closed. It had sizzled away. The Dragon's Gate was gone. I have not seen my little brothers since that day."

Lumea and Viorica asked no more questions. The Taniwha was very upset by her own story. Viorica wrapped a sympathetic wing around Kari's spine-covered back. The three of them were silent for several minutes.

Finally, Lumea thought aloud. "Now I understand why it's called the Dragon's Gate. It takes away Dragons only. Even ocean waters can't flow into its void."

Viorica and Lumea slowly turned their heads and looked into each other's eyes. They had the same thought. Would they ever see their friends again?

6-Reunion

Tanarul and Ayo had been given two assignments in their quest for Dragon's Gate information. Their first trip to Hawaii had been successful. Kihawahine's story was now filed away in the vaults of total recall. Dragon's memories are so detail-oriented that they never have to take notes or dictate them when they have one of the human's devices. As on all their journeys, Tanarul also made precise drawings of every new Dragon he met.

The two young Dragons were airborne and nearing Australia opposite the coast from the Tasmania side. They were to interview the Mindi, a Serpent-Dragon relative of Bertie the Bunyip. The Yarra Yarra people often referred to the Mindi as the Bunyip Snake. This particular Mindi was named Mort. He lived in the depths of a large freshwater lake, the home of most Bunyips. However, Ayo and Tanarul were just one of the first visiting Dragons to arrive.

The swift Hai Riyo and his passenger had reached Maui shortly after Kihawahine had said goodbye to her visitors. She informed them that Tanarul had mentioned their next stop would be in northwestern Australia, where they would interview the Mindi. About four minutes later, the Hai Riyo had no problem reaching Mort's lake.

The Hai Riyo, Shou, had slowed down for a soft landing to allow Urk to hop off onto the ground before him. Urk had kept his eyes closed, his wings folded, and his feet and claws tightly wrapped around Shou's feather-like scales for the entire ride. He had appreciated the ride but had no desire to travel that fast again for the rest of his life. He immediately jumped from Shou's back and collapsed on the ground.

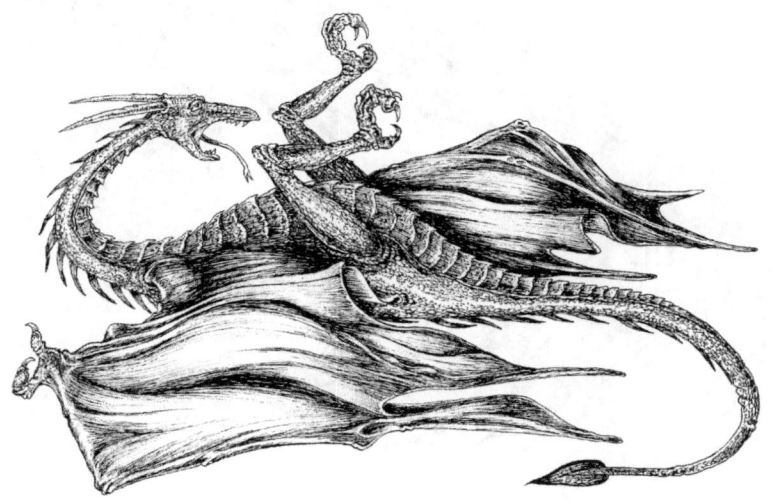

"I don't know what I can ever do to repay you for the half-a-world tour you just gave me," said Urk.

"You would have enjoyed it even more with your eyes open," said Shou.

"I was on your back all the way. How did you know my eyes were closed?" asked Urk.

"My passengers always close their eyes!" Shou laughed, "and your offer to repay me is not necessary. Helping friends is my reward, but now that we are here at the lake, I cannot direct you to the home of an underwater Dragon."

"I should have no problem finding the Mindi," said Urk. "When I last visited Australia, I learned how to imitate the bellow of a baby Bunyip! Now that I have grown to this size, I'm sure I have the lung capacity to yell loud enough."

"Ah yes, Bunyip bellows are thunderous," said Shou, "and they inspire me to use my gift of flying faster than the speed of sound. Happy hunting, friend Urk."

As always, the Hai Riyo had disappeared, stirring up a strong breeze and leaving Urk clinging to a nearby bamboo shoot for balance. He now had the chance to test out his new volume. None of the three heads of the Balaur had made a sound when they had instructed him on fire control. He had known other fire-breathers to be extremely vocal when they spewed out their display.

Sound effects always heightened the drama. Urk practiced the baby Bunyip below at a low volume a few times for quality. He then took a deep breath and let out an echoing cry so loud that the volume surprised him and sent him tumbling backward over a large rock.

A baby Bunyip bellow sounds like a combination of a tuba's most resounding note and a rattling bucket of nails, beautiful only to an elder Bunyip. As Urk wobbled back to his feet and peered over the rock, he saw that his efforts were already causing a reaction beneath the waters. A few bubbles were joined by a few more. The surface began to churn.

Finally, the lake waters formed a small whirlpool, gradually winding to a center where the bubble activity became more furious. Urk knew that the Mindi was about to appear. He started to unfurl his wings to fly high enough for the massive creature to see him, but he quickly changed his mind and ducked back behind the rock.

He had switched his attention to the sky. Two familiar silhouettes had appeared against the sun: a winged Dragon descending very quickly and a wingless one holding tightly to the flyer's tail. Sticking his head out even lower and to the side of the rock, he was mostly hidden by some tall grass. Urk quickly ducked into hiding again as Ayo and Tanarul descended to the lake's shore. The two young Dragons immediately noticed the water churning and bubbling.

"What good luck!" Tanarul exclaimed. "Maybe we won't have to dive into the lake after all to find the Mindi."

Ayo was thrilled. Like all winged dragons, he disliked getting his wings soaked.

Mort, the Mindi, wasted no time making his presence known, causing a great splash as his head and a generous link of his serpentine body came into full view. He was bobbing up and down as he spoke. "G' day, mates! Dragons from afar, I see. Which one of you called to me using that baby Bunyip bellow? That impression was ripper! Almost had me fooled!"

"What's 'ripper'?" whispered Ayo.

"I think it means very good or maybe great," Tanarul whispered.

Mort immediately switched to Dragon Speak, the universal language of Dragons.

"Not familiar with the local color?" he said. "I'm surprised since one of you certainly mastered the language of the young ones of my family."

"Neither of us speaks, Baby Bunyip," said Tanarul. "I am not educated in your speech patterns at all. The last time I was here, I had an Urkind Dragon in my ear. He is a skilled interpreter."

Behind the rock, Urk was urged to hop up and yell, "Surprise!" But he held back.

"I am Tanarul of Romania," continued the young Dragon.

"And I am Ayo of Kilimanjaro! The Great Red Dragon of the South sent us. We are looking for information about the Dragon's Gate."

"Sent by Chilong?" asked Mort. "Yours must be an important mission, but all I know of the Dragon's Gate is Ancient History."

"All history is as valuable as we will allow it to be," said Tanarul.

The Bunyip Serpent paused and looked at Tanarul for a moment. "You're from Romania...one of the Great Lumea Veche's students?'

"How did you know?" asked Tanarul.

"Lucky guess," smiled Mort.

"A Dragon's Gate has appeared recently and swallowed up some of our friends," Ayo urgently reported.

"Well, that's a Dragon Horse of a different color," said Mort. "A dire situation. I thought the Gates had closed permanently. They are energy surges that open holes in the atmosphere we breathe. No Dragon knows what causes them, and very few of us have ever seen one."

"But you have seen one?" asked Ayo.

"Yes...let's see...about twelve thousand years ago," Mort sadly answered. "It was a foggy void to nowhere. It opened from its center, and a bright light framed its circumference. It appeared in the middle of a rare gathering of different species of Dragons in this area now called Australia. We were troubled by the disappearance of the giant Ice Age wombat. The poor animal was not adapting well to the coming climate change, and we were discussing how a Dragon might help them survive.

Unfortunately, firebreathers could do little about making the climate colder. Our meeting was in the process of breaking up. Then, the phenomenon the Chinese Dragons call the Dragon's Gate appeared. Several Dragons were immediately drawn into it and disappeared. Then, it began to rotate as if mounted to the side of a wheel. More Dragons were sucked into the void. The rest of us quickly crawled, ran, or flew out of its range. I was not drawn toward it for some reason, but I joined the others in their retreat.

"I wonder why you weren't attracted to it?" asked Tanarul.

"I still don't have a clue about that," answered the Mindi. "But to continue, the sky was filled with light for a second as several streams of lightning shot over our heads, but there was no thunder. I think the lightning might have shot from the closing gate's center. We saw it pass over our heads, but it never touched the ground. When we looked back where the gate had been, it was gone. It took 17 Dragons with it that day, none of my serpent dragon family, but many other species."

"It's even more dangerous than we imagined!" declared Tanarul. "It can sweep around sucking in Dragons like a vacuum cleaner!"

"A what?" asked Mort.

"It's a human-made device that removes dirt," said Ayo.

"Why would anyone want to remove dirt?" asked Mort.

"That's one of those human mysteries we'll probably never solve," Tanarul answered, "but our problem right now is the mystery of the Dragon's Gate."

"I doubt my story will be of much help to you," said the Mindi. "We have been unable to figure out what happened to our friends for thousands of years."

"But you let us know more about the Gate's power," said Ayo. "If these voids keep appearing, they could vacuum up every Dragon on the planet!"

Urk could remain hidden no longer. "We've got to stop them!" he yelled, flapping into midair from behind the rock.

Ayo and Tanarul froze. They recognized the voice and the determined attitude of their good friend Urk, but this Dragon was many times his size. The two friends looked at each other and quickly back at Urk.

"Are you...?" asked Tanarul.

"You couldn't forget your old friend, Urk, could you?" asked the tiny hovering Dragon.

"Of course not! There is only one explanation. Hibernation seems to have magnified you!"

"It doesn't stop with size!" said Urk. He reached down, picked up the huge rock that had hidden him, and threw it directly toward Ayo's head. Ayo swung around, and smoke started streaming from his nostrils, but Urk had sent a blast of his fire breath to do the job himself before he could reduce the rock to a cinder.

"Fire breath!" said Tanarul. "That would make you a Greater..."

"A Greater Lesser Dragon, I suppose," reasoned Urk. "I haven't figured myself out yet."

"I'm sure of one thing about you," said Tanarul, "that you are here and back in our lives. No more labels are required."

"I'm sure of something about your friend, too," said the Mindi. "He is very skilled at imitating baby Bunyip bellows. Since neither of you knew what a Bunyip below is, Urk is the only other candidate."

"I thought it might lure you out of the lake," said Urk. "I hope you will forgive my joke."

"Something else is different about Urk," whispered Ayo to Tanarul. "He's polite."

"My hearing is much better, too, Ayo," smiled Urk.

"And I also know why Urk was here tempting Mort to the surface, Ayo," said Tanarul. "He didn't want you to have to get your wings wet."

"I'm loving the new Urk," said Ayo.

"Lucian must have told you where we would probably be, Urk. Has your speed also increased so you can fly to Australia?" asked Tanarul.

"Lucian also arranged for Hai Riyo express," said Urk. "We traced your trip from Romania to Maui and to here."

"We're glad to have you join us, Urk, even though you must be twelve times bigger!" said Ayo.

Urk grinned, "Well, only eight times, but who's counting?"

"Where is your next stop?" asked Mort.

"Shangri-La," said Tanarul.

"I thought that was a myth," said Mort.

"Only to humans," said Tanarul. "So many don't want to think we exist either."

"Humans are so serious, especially adult humans," said Urk. "They need to have more fun."

Shou, the swift Hai Riyo, delivered regular progress reports to Lucian, Vladimir, and Phoebe. "Lumea and Viorica have contacted the Taniwha and successfully gathered information from her. After their trip to Maui, Tanarul and Ayo interviewed the Australian Mindi, who were also joined by Urk. All of them are now on their way to Shangri-La." Shou then left as quickly as he had arrived.

"I wanted to ask him how Tanarul and Ayo reacted to the super-sized Urk," said Lucian, "but the Hai Riyo are always gone so suddenly."

"That's their job," said Phoebe.

"It's a good time to continue work on your book of Dragons," said Vladimir, "since we can't do anything about finding Bogdan from here."

Lucian eagerly grabbed his tablet and the stack of Tanarul's drawings. It was easier to look at the originals since he was making notes on his tablet.

"Those drawings depict what some human researchers call 'lower dragons,'" said Vladimir, "but their sincere research has been without the benefit of Dragon assistance. That one would be classified as a Lindorm. This is Sven, Lindorm of Sweden. That is where most of their species originated in Europe. As you can see, he is a Serpent Dragon with the addition of arms. The human tales have them shooting venom instead of fire, but Sven would tell you that isn't true.

Humans have written that listening to soft music makes most Lindorms weakened and tamed from their evil ways. They like soft music as much as you and I, but their ways were never evil in the first place.

Vladimir continued. "That drawing is of what humans call a Wyvern. When we discussed this earlier, I mentioned that a bat-winged Dragon like me might be called a Wyvern. This is how people pictured them on their shields and armor in those long-ago days. Their Wyvern is serpent-like, with legs and a set of wings. There are many Wyvern myths and fables. Some of the yarns tell us that they are outraged by the color red, have thick scales, and can be killed only by a sword plunged directly into their navels."

"Their navels?" asked Lucian. "But aren't all Dragons..."

"Hatched from eggs?" said Vladimir. "You can judge for yourself the degree of truth in that story. The following picture is a type of dragon we discussed earlier, too. The people of Great Britain classified it as a Worm, although we Dragons prefer the spelling WYRM. It separates them from the earthworms, which are beneficial creatures, but they are not Dragons.

The Wyrms are of great length and are fire breathers, even though humans reported that they spewed out clouds of poisonous gas instead of fire. The gas clouds could wipe out the plant life in their fields or even in whole valleys.

This is why many droughts in the old stories were falsely blamed on Dragons. We may not have the freshest breath on the planet, but it's not poisonous. The Wyrms are usually not very chatty, and little is known of their origin. Maybe you can interview one someday and get the whole story.

"I would love to interview a Wyrm!" said Lucian.

"You are a pretty charming fellow," said Phoebe, "the type of guy a Wyrm would consider good company."

Lucian smiled broadly. Most people would have thought Phoebe's statement offensive, but Lucian considered it the highest of compliments.

While Ayo was busy talking with Mort, the Mindi, Tanarul, asked Urk a few questions. "Why were you hiding from us earlier, Urk? You must have known we would be glad to see you."

"I wasn't hiding from the two of you," Urk answered. "I was hiding from you."

"From me?" asked a surprised Tanarul. "Why would you ever hide from me? You have given me the best advice and comedy relief I've ever had, and you know Dragons never forget."

"I thought you would be disappointed that I won't be able to fit in your ear anymore," said Urk. "We've had so many good times together, and now that's all over."

"Urk, every Dragon grows, one way or another," said Tanarul. "If we didn't, we would fade into boring myths again. We shouldn't just be willing to change. We should expect change and welcome it."

"Such wisdom! Did you change into Lumea while I was hibernating?" laughed Urk.

Now, both Dragons were laughing. "I see some things about you will never change; the best things!" said Tanarul.

Ayo joined them as the Mindi slithered back into his water home. "Are you two ready for Shangri-La?"

Urk and Tanarul agreed that they were.

As the three of them took to the sky, Tanarul looked at Urk, who was now flying beside his ear. "Urk, my old friend, you may not be able to fit in my ear anymore, but you'll always be in my head!"

7-Shangri-La

A few minutes later, as the three Dragons were joined in flight by Viorica and Lumea, Tanarul kept sorting out the facts in his mind. "A void to nowhere opened by a beam of light...lightning without thunder...never striking the ground...opening clockwise...did that really matter?" He was anxious to hear the Taniwha's story from Lumea and Viorica after they had landed at their destination near Tibet. He also kept glancing toward the rising mountains.

He remembered visiting the hidden fog-covered valleys of the highest mountain range in the world, the Himalayas, somewhere just north of there. Living there was the Great Behemoth, the largest Dragon who still walked the earth. Their whole party could easily fit in his ear. That had been the experience that had made Tanarul even more aware of how it must feel to be a Lesser Dragon.

As they reached the country of Bhutan, Viorica and Lumea picked up speed and began to circle down to their destination in a hidden green field. The others followed. Neither of the older Dragons had registered any surprise at all about Urk's increase in size after hibernation. "I'm so excited to be able to see you better," said Viorica. "My eyes are not as trained as Lumea's."

"So, you're not surprised that a Lesser Dragon can grow eight times larger?" asked Urk.

"I've seen Dragons sometimes sprout wings or grow an extra head or two during hibernation," said Lumea. "Nothing shocks me."

"I just met one of those Dragons who added a third head, and she taught me how to control this..."

Urk shot a long and powerful stream of fire at a large tree stump, turning it into excellent charcoal for some human's compost pile.

Lumea's eyes opened wide. "Nothing shocks me, but that! I have never known a Lesser Dragon to develop the ability to breathe fire!"

Viorica clapped her folded wingtips together. "Delightful! I haven't heard of that either. And, for the first time in my life, I've seen Lumea surprised! What a gift you are, Urk."

"Urk had shown us the truth in what Tanarul has been saying all along," said Lumea.

Tanarul quickly became very interested in the conversation.

"Since Urk is now a fire-breather, and an excellent one by the way, he can no longer be classified as a Lesser Dragon," Lumea continued, "but, since he has not yet achieved the full height requirement, he can't be called a Greater. Those rules are now ridiculous!"

"So, what am I?" asked Urk.

"You are a Dragon!" Lumea answered. "Tanarul has insisted to all of us that a Dragon is a Dragon, no matter how big, no matter how small. Now, you have proven to us that the terms 'Lesser' and 'Greater' no longer have any meaning...if they ever did! When we find Bogdan, the first subject we must discuss in council is abandoning those labels for all time."

"So, would I have to be serious and really smart like a Greater Dragon?" asked Urk.

"No labels, remember? Your only requirement would be to continue being Urk!" said Viorica. Being true to yourself is the best prescription this Doctor can give you."

Urk knew that Viorica was the most respected of all Dragon physicians and she would never make a declaration like that lightly. He stood up straight and put his winged arms on his hips. "I think I'm cured, Doc!"

Tanarul and Ayo were beaming with joy. Urk was himself again and Lumea was finally convinced that the divisive labels of an earlier generation didn't work anymore. However, everyone there knew that the real celebration would have to come later.

"Now we must share our Dragon's Gate information before Druk of Bhutan arrives," Lumea announced. "The Dragon Horse caught us mid-flight on our way back from New Zealand. He said Druk had been informed of our visit and would quickly be meeting us in the center of this vast green valley where we just landed."

After the essential facts were shared, Tanarul began asking questions. "According to the Taniwha, was there thunder with the lightning?"

"She didn't mention any," said Viorica.

"Both Mort and Kihawahine mentioned its absence," said Tanarul. "Since the Taniwha said nothing about thunder, it's safe to guess there wasn't any."

"Lightning that travels in a straight path over the horizon makes no sense to me," said Urk.

"Nor to me," Lumea agreed.

"Mort said that of the seventeen Dragons whisked away in Australia, none of them was a Serpent Dragon," said Ayo.

"Curious," said Viorica, "but the part of his story that was the creepiest was about the Gate acting like a vacuum and cleaning the place out of Dragons."

"And only Dragons," Lumea said. "When the Taniwha told us that the Dragon's Gate rose to the surface of the ocean, and yet, none of the water was sucked into it, we knew that Dragons alone were the prey."

"Did either of them mention that the Gate opened clockwise?" asked Tanarul.

The other Dragons shook their heads. "Why is that detail important?" asked Urk.

"Every detail is important," Lumea answered.

"Why did I know he would say that?" asked Ayo.

Lumea grinned. "Because you know me too well, the mark of a good student."

"Speaking of good students, where exactly are we?" asked Urk.

"We are in a small country the humans have named Bhutan. It's a small nation wedged in the middle of China, Tibet, and India," said Lumea. "The Dragon we are about to meet is a national hero here. They consider him their protector. He is also called the Thunder Dragon. The powerful rolls of thunder that echo through these rocky canyons are said to be caused by their mighty protector. Druk's picture is proudly featured on their flag."

"And this open field is Shangri-La?" asked Urk. "I thought it was like some sort of paradise on earth. This is a nice field, but not my idea of paradise."

"I know very little about Shangri-La," Lumea answered. "All I can tell you is that it was first mentioned in a book written by a human in the early 20th century, so it is not the ancient city many people think it to be."

"Is it a real place?" asked Ayo.

"Like many human stories, it may be a combination of several places. I believe Druk will be able to answer these questions much better than I can," said Lumea.

"We may have our answers soon," said Tanarul. "Here he comes."

Viorica leaped into the sky, flying in a small circle to guide Druk to their location. He was a sky swimmer, like many of the Dragons in that part of the world. His picture on the country's flag was not a bad likeness. He even carried the four huge round jewels depicted on the nation's symbol.

Druk flew a few circular laps above them with Viorica before the two of them landed. As he spoke, he juggled the four huge jewels to amuse himself. "Greetings, Dragons of Romania...and Africa, too," said Druk. The Horse Dragon has told me the sad story of why you are visiting. Since you are here, I presume you are still in search of Dragon's Gate clues."

"You presume right, your Thundership!" said Urk, trying to think of a respectful name for the Dragon of Thunder.

"I'll show you how I make it later if you like," said Druk, giving a slight bow to the little Dragon. "I suppose you would also like to know the location of Shangri-La?"

"We are honored that you would take time out of your busy schedule to help us," said Lumea.

"Busy?" asked Druk. "It doesn't even look like rain. I'm at your service. Let's take a tour. The Dragon's Gate event happened in Shangri-La."

"Shall we fly?" asked Viorica and Ayo in unison, already hovering above the tall grass.

"Follow me," said Druk.

As the six of them flapped or sailed, the Dragon of Thunder showed them points of interest along the way. "You can see that the humans here take very good care of their city. They have built many multi-level dwellings on the steps of these steep cliffs. Other humans find them sort of magical-looking, I suppose. Oh, there's a Shangri-La sign on that one."

"It's that easy to find?" asked Tanarul.

"That's the Shangri-La Hotel," laughed Druk. "Over there, that's the Shangri-La Health Spa or something similar. Up ahead is the Shangri-La Ski Shop. There are lots of tourist attractions all over the town with that name. In this part of Asia, people name everything after their mystical little village where people are said to have lived for hundreds of years."

Even though they were flying very high, Ayo asked, "Shouldn't we be Chameleon-cloaked?"

"Be my guest," Druk answered. The tourists here will just suppose we are kites, though. They're used to being entertained. "Ah, there's the Shangri-La Gym and Vegan Bar."

"You are taking us to the Real Shangri-La, aren't you?" inquired Urk.

"Assuredly," said Druk, "the only one that is important to Dragons. That's where the Dragon's Gate incident occurred."

The winged Dragons suddenly lost their rhythms and hovered a few seconds from the slightly shocking news. They quickly recovered their stride.

"When we are about to approach the mountain pass where it's located, you'll quickly see why it's impossible for humans to ever find it." Druk continued.

They continued to sail in winding paths through steep canyons, rock formations, and expanses of tall fir tree forests. Leaving the very elaborate architecture of the resorts behind them, now all they saw were only a few scattered small villages.

"Are we still in Bhutan?" asked Tanarul.

"I've never paid much attention to borders out here," said Druk. "Who knows? People are always naming things they pretend they own. These cliffs and mountains are too rugged for their dwellings. There are no minerals here that they would want to steal."

"Their human Shangri-La is a place where those things don't matter, though," said Viorica, "and where they can escape the pressures they inflict on themselves. When I look at these tiny, isolated settlements, I think any of them could be Shangri-La."

"Maybe one of them is," said Druk, "but called by another name, I'm sure. None of those villagers would have read the book or seen the movies."

"The further away we get from the main cities, I've begun to notice an increase in the number of Padure Dragons in these vast forests," Lumea commented.

"Only the Great Lumea Veche would be aware of that," said Druk. "This area holds probably the largest concentration of those wonderful Tree-Dragons on the planet."

"You said that this Dragon Shangri-La is a place that would be impossible for humans to ever discover. I am beginning to understand why," said Lumea.

"I'm beginning to wonder if it's a place Dragons can find either!" said Ayo, who was getting tired of the tour. He was a Dragon of action who had been amusing himself by flying in an occasional cartwheel or quick dive along the way."

"Your patience is about to be rewarded, Ayo," said Druk. There's the entrance up ahead."

They descended into a rugged area with high vertical canyon walls on each side. There were dozens of very high chimney rock formations jutting out of the heavily wooded canyon floor. Some were eroded at their bottoms, leaving rock awnings hanging over the trees and other shorter chimney rocks. The area described as the entrance was solidly packed with tall trees crowded closely together.

"Entrance?" asked Urk. "Those trees are growing so close to each other, even I couldn't fly between them."

"Trees?" asked Lumea.

Immediately, all Lumea's companions could see what Lumea's one-word question meant. "Padures!" exclaimed Tanarul, "a whole forest of them. That's why this place will always be impossible for humans to locate or record. In remote locations like this, they mark their trails by tying objects to trees. That system works only when the trees don't decide to get up and go for a walk."

"The Great Tanarul is right, of course," said Druk. "Every evening, the members of the Padure forest deliberately switch positions or take strolls to visit another grove in the next valley. Every morning, this is a completely different landscape."

One of the tallest of the Dragon trees joined in the conversation, her voice melodious like wind whistling through a hollow log, "Welcome to Dragon Shangri-La!" On cue, the forest began moving, gradually stepping aside to the left and right. None of the visitors had seen so many Padures gathered in one place before. It was a spectacular sight, even for a Dragon. Eventually, the Dragon trees had carved out a wide, winding path to the heart of the canyon floor.

An archway rock marked the true entrance to the rather enchanted-looking location. It was a high arch, high enough for very tall Dragons. Taller ones could simply step or fly over it. Passing through the arch, they were surprised to see the vastness of the area. The flat-topped chimney rocks were everywhere, giving the appearance of high buildings in a small city.

That was where the resemblance to civilization ended. Dragons had no use for elaborate structures with carved decorations and tile roofs. They could survive in any climate. Neither did they need to live in a magical land where the atmosphere would prolong their lives. Most of them already had life expectancies of hundreds of thousands of years. Some celebrated their birthdays in the millions.

Urk had flown through the arch with glee. Like a bat feasting in a swarm of insects, he flitted in and out of natural windows in the towering rocks and caves along the cliffs. To him, it truly was a highly inquisitive little Dragon's paradise.

In the distance, Viorica and Ayo discovered a winding stream fed by several towering waterfalls. Fish were jumping out of the fresh water, and the trees were full of colorful singing birds. Urk eventually joined them there.

"Are those fish and birds cyborgs?" asked Urk. "I'm not believin' this place."

As Lumea and Tanarul, led by Druk, walked down the path, taking in the sights, other Dragons often popped into view.

Lumea, who had been traveling the world for a few million years, recognized several of them as old friends.

Tanarul had been doing a lot of traveling himself in the last several years. Some of the Dragons were familiar faces to him as well.

"We appreciate the tour, Druk," said Tanarul, "but can you direct us to some of the Dragons who witnessed the Dragon's Gate event? Did it happen in this beautiful valley?"

"Ah, the Dragon Horse said that you would be anxious to get down to the reason for your visit," said Druk. "Yes, the Dragon's Gate did appear here, in this very location, and I would suggest you ask questions of anyone you see. To my knowledge, every Dragon here witnessed it."

Thank you," said Tanarul. "Who do you suggest we ask, Lumea?"

Lumea scanned the area. "Well, the Bixi sunning herself on that rock is an old friend. Let's see what she might have to offer."

The Bixi is a Chinese Dragon that looks like a tortoise with a Dragon's head. They are popular symbols of endurance in carrying heavy loads and long life.

Lumea approached his old friend. "Lin, it is good to see you again. I have admired your majestic new statue in Forbidden City. Have you seen it?"

"Lumea! Your visits are always welcome. I have not seen the statue you mentioned, but I will trust your review. What brings you to Dragon Shangri-La? By the way, I love the atmosphere, but I can't stand the name. Can you?"

"It could use some work," Lumea answered. "My young friend, Tanarul, and some other companions are here gathering information on the Dragon's Gate appearance here in the valley. Can you describe what you saw?"

"Yes, it was a circle of light with a void behind it. It appeared just beyond those waterfalls. Seven Dragons near it appeared to want to leap into it, and they did. Then the circle closed on itself, and it was gone."

"Can you tell us anything else about it?" asked Tanarul.

"A point of the light from the edge seemed to be closing on itself until it disappeared into its center."

"In which direction did it spin?"

"Clockwise," said Lin.

"Did horizontal lightning spew out of its center?" asked Tanarul.

"It did, but I saw it very well from this distance," she answered. "It was almost as fast as lightning, but it arched a few times like a crawling snake as it crossed the sky and disappeared."

"Was it just one strand of light?" Tanarul continued.

"Oh no, there were seven flashes," said Lin. "Why do you ask?"

"I'm not sure why at this point," said Tanarul. "We're just gathering all the details we can. Some friends disappeared through a Dragon's Gate, and we're here trying to figure out how to get them back."

"If they want to come back," said Lin. "The ones from here seemed very willing to go."

This thought had never occurred to Tanarul or any of the others. What if Bogdan and Chen had left willingly?

Lumea and Tanarul thanked Lin for her report and continued strolling the garden, talking to several other of Lumea's old friends who were relaxing in the beautiful retreat. Ayo, Viorica, and Urk also had spent the rest of the afternoon getting the same story from a number of other Dragon witnesses. There was no variation in even one detail. Finally, they met Druk back at the Archway Rock.

"I believe we have gathered all the information here that we can get, Druk," said Lumea. "I suppose we will be heading back to Romania to discuss the next step with friends there."

"Another important detail came up!" said Urk. None of them likes the name 'Dragon Shangri-La.'"

"That name needs some re-thinking. Come back when you want to spend a little time in Paradise...no, that doesn't work either...Valhala...no..." said Druk.

Everyone wished him luck in coming up with a name for perfection and thanked him for his help. When Urk took his turn, he added, "But wait! We're not through here. You said you would show us how you make thunder, Great Thunder Dragon!"

"Do you have time? "Asked Druk.

"I know I do!" said Ayo. "I'm still waiting for this trip's adventure to begin!

"Follow me," said Druk. He took off to a nearby rock canyon with very high vertical walls and positioned all his friends along the ledge like sporting event fans. He then picked up all four huge round jewels he always had by his side, one in each vast, clawed hand and foot. He once again looked like the Thunder Dragon on Bhutan's flag. He sprang up and sky-swam a great distance past the end of the long canyon.

Turning to build-up speed, Druk dived toward the center of the long canyon. The other Dragons could see that he was holding all four jewels straight out of his body. Entering the canyon at full speed, he began crashing the jewels together and rolling them quickly against each other. The result was the echoing canyon sounds of the loudest thunderclaps any of his applauding audience had ever heard. They were shaking like the boulders around them. He flew back into the sky and repeated variations of the echoing noise several times; each time, echo covering echo. The effect increased in volume. Druk, indeed, was the Thunder Dragon.

As the five Dragons took to the sky and headed toward Romania, they passed again over the small town they had first seen on their trip. Chameleon-cloaked this time, they descended for a better view. There was a long line outside one of the stores. The Dragons turned to each other, laughing as they read the sign above its door: Shangri-La Umbrella Shop.

8-The Gate

Lucian sat in front of his laptop with two small Dragons on each side. They were not small because they were Lesser Dragons. They were young Greater Dragons who would someday be taller than Vladimir but were now about half the height of their human friend. Fetita was a spine-winged Dragon. Prunk had webbed finger-wings like a bat, the same as Vladimir and Viorica.

"We're learning as much about Wyrms from you as we've learned from Vladimir," said Fetita.

"Maybe even more," said her friend Prunk.

"No one can tell more Dragon Stories than Vladimir," replied Lucian, "but when he told me that no one knows much about the origin of Wyrms, I decided to research some of the stories humans tell about them. Look at this one. It's from a Dr. Bunny Campbell in the U. S. She's a member of the Human/Dragon Alliance.

They turned their attention to the screen. Lucian began to scroll down several pictures of Dragons native to North America. All of them were Wyrms. He paused on one with incredibly long tusks.

"This one is said to live in a State called Arkansas," Lucian explained. "He is called a Gowrow, a huge water snake according to Native American legends, but Dr.

Campbell reports that the Gowrow is a fire-breathing Dragon. He is a Wyrm, spelled with a "Y," to be exact, but the Americans usually spell it Worm with an 'O'."

"Why do humans spell the same words in different ways?" asked Fetita.

"Lots of reasons," Lucian answered. "We have so many languages and so much division that people in different countries develop special ways they like to see words spelled. Look at this."

He showed the two young Dragons a map of the United States. "The State where Gowrow lives is called Arkansas. It ends with 'SAS,' but they pronounce it 'Arkan-saw.'"

Prunk studied the map. "Here's another state with that name...well, almost that name. It's called 'Kan-saw.'"

"the people of that State call it 'Kan-sas.'"

"But aren't those two States part of the same country?" asked Prunk. "I thought you said only people of different countries pronounced the same word in different ways."

"The people of that country have lots of different ideas about what is right," said Lucian.

"I guess that's why it's divided up into fifty States!" said Fetita.

"That's a good point," said Lucian thoughtfully, "but the subject we're talking about right now is American Wyrms."

"With an "O,'" added Prunk.

Vladimir and Phoebe had been away for a few hours to celebrate the latest rebirth from fire at the nearby Phoenix flock.

"Your flock always inspires me," said Vladimir as the two of them approached Lucian and the young Dragons. "Whenever we watch our lives literally go up in flames, we know hope is always waiting to be born."

Phoebe lit on a rock near Lucian. "And not just in my family," Phoebe replied. "I get the same feeling from yours. What is a more hopeful sight than Fetita and Prunk learning from our bright young human friend?"

"How many lives did it take you to learn how to be such a flatterer?" laughed Lucian.

Phoebe smiled as well as a bird can with their hard beak. "About 512, I suppose."

"Any word from Shangri-La?" asked Vladimir.

"Some Human/Dragon Alliance members in Tibet texted that our friends are on their way home," Lucian replied. "Urk has joined them. They should be back in a couple of hours, but there is still no sign of Bogdan. Meanwhile. I've been doing some more research on Wyrms. I've learned a few new details."

"Yes!" exclaimed Prunk. "Did you know some people in the U.S. spell the word 's-a-s' but pronounce it 'saw'?"

"An interesting discovery," said Vladimir. "Am I to presume one of the Wyrms you are studying lives in Arkansas?"

"Vladimir's a genius, Prunk," said Fetita.

Vladimir agreed with her. "I have not heard of any Wyrm stories from that part of the world. Your research seems to be paying off."

"I have a list of Wyrms from all over the States," said Lucian proudly. "My friend, Dr. Campbell, has gathered information from several original tribes there for years. All their stories have been repeated for centuries by word-of-mouth until now."

"Most of the Wyrms in the States live in the deep lakes and rivers. They keep to themselves," said Vladimir. "The stories of the Native People have always been the best sources to let us know that the Wyrms exist at all. Your book will be valuable to all of us, Lucian."

"I wish I could be more valuable in the search for Bogdan!" said Lucian, "but here I sit, researching Wyrms, while my friends fly around the world doing all the important work."

"Any work done well is important work," said Vladimir. "Who knows how much your research will teach us someday?"

"Well, I do have a pretty long list of Wyrms I would like to interview in the future, but they're all over the world," said Lucian.

"No doubt some flights can be arranged for you after Bogdan is back among us," said Vladimir.

Lucian's eyes sparkled as he remembered the single time he had been aboard a flying Dragon. Ayo had given him a ride during their search for clues when they were on the trail of the Dragon-Man. The memory of that thrill made him forget for several blissful moments all about Wyrms, Dragon's Gates, and web searches.

"Mr. Lucian, Mr. Lucian," said Fetita, "are you feeling OK?

"What?" Lucian shook his head. "I'm good...just thinking about flying...and you don't have to call me Mister. After all, you're both a lot older than I am."

He was right. The two young Dragons were each around 50 years old but nowhere near fully grown. An average Dragon's lifespan could easily be several hundred thousand years old.

"Always welcome respect, Lucian," said Phoebe. "It's a rare gift these days in your world."

Lucian had to agree.

"Look... up in the sky!" shouted Prunk.

Four familiar shapes were high above the clouds, and now, they were fading into sight as they eased away their Chameleon Cloaking. Ayo was in the lead, followed by Viorica's broader soaring wings. Lumea and Tanarul then emerged, riding the mighty wind currents of their friends. As the party grew nearer, a fifth Dragon appeared, the much smaller but still magnified silhouette of Urk.

After they landed and greetings had been exchanged, Prunk and Fetita could not stop marveling at Urk's greatly expanded size.

"Will we grow up that quickly, too?' asked Fetita.

"I doubt it," said Urk, "but I was already grown up when I was the size of a mouse. I just got augmented a bit during hibernation. Don't ask me why."

"Is being augmented fun?" asked Prunk.

"It can be," Urk answered, "but I can't fit into Tanarul's ear anymore. I'll miss that, but I can breathe fire now!"

"Cool!" said Prunk.

"It's pretty hot," said Urk as he shot a narrow stream of flames that made a medium-sized rock glow red at Fetita's feet. She immediately bent over and picked it up, tossing it back and forth with Prunk.

Lucian had flinched at first as she had picked up the glowing rock, momentarily forgetting that Dragons are immune to their own heat.

Everyone else was listening to their various reports, led mostly by Lumea and Tanarul, as they summed up the results of their findings in Hawaii, the South Pacific, and Bhutan. Ayo, Viorica, and Urk added further details to their discoveries about the Dragon's Gate events.

"Streaks of lightning that never strike the ground?" mused Vladimir, "and they just disappear over the horizon?"

"And the gate itself, opening up like a big round hole in the sky?" asked Lucian. "In the human world, that sounds like a wormhole...the kind of thing I've seen in sci-fi movies. They're like entrances to another time or a parallel Universe."

"Yes," said Viorica, "exactly like that! A gateway to another world. That's how The Dragon's Gates were described to us. Tell us more about Worm Holes."

"Well," said Lucian, "I'm no expert, but I believe they're one of the theories discussed in what humans call Quantum Physics."

"What's Quantum Physics, Mr. Lucian?" asked Fetita.

"I'm a human, but I'm not a scientist," said Lucian. "There are a lot of theories in Quantum Science, sort of a completely different way to look at the sciences we already know about, but it's all theories, nothing proven so far. Here, let me show you..."

Lucian tapped a few keys on his laptop, and the entire group of Dragons, one human and one Phoenix, gathered around the small screen for a view. They read about sub-atomic particles and saw many diagrams of how wormholes might appear: two funnels faced opposite directions with smaller ends connected in the middle.

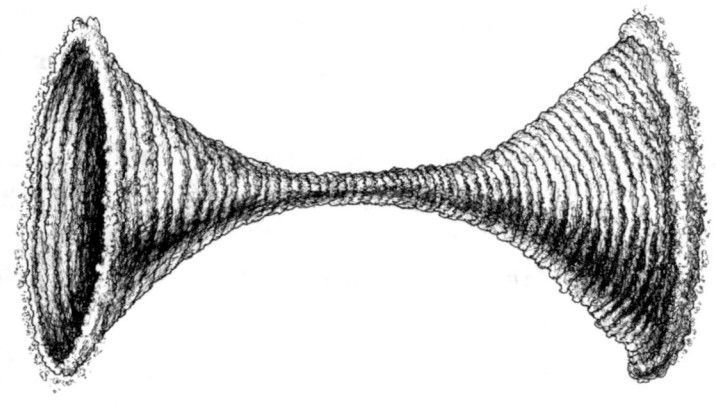

"Do these wormholes open up from a small point of light in their middle?" asked Lucian.

"And get bigger and bigger as they spiral open?" asked Ayo.

"Do streaks of light shoot out of them?" asked Viorica.

"Are they available in a selection of colors?" asked Urk.

At this point, everyone stopped asking questions and stared at Urk for several seconds. Only the Phoenix squawked with a little laughter. The questions resumed.

"Do they close up clockwise or counterclockwise?" asked Tanarul.

"As I understand it, no human has ever seen a wormhole. To your people, they're just a theory at this point. Am I correct?" asked Lumea.

"That is correct, Great Lumea," said Lucian.

"But maybe someone has seen them," said Viorica, "except that someone has never been a human but has always been a Dragon!"

"And this object humans are very recently defining as a wormhole is what our species has been calling a Dragon's Gate for thousands of years," concluded Vladimir.

"Holy Hologram!" exclaimed Urk.

"What?" asked Tanarul.

"It's something I heard on a TV show once. I just wanted to contribute to the conversation," said Urk, meekly.

"It's always good to uh...join in, Urk," said Lumea.

"Then I have a question," said Fetita. "Is worm spelled with an 'o' or a 'y'?"

The others chuckled a little and Vladimir patted Fetita on the head; but suddenly Tanarul stopped chuckling and exclaimed, "With a 'y'? Fetita could have just solved the puzzle. What if these things are not wormholes at all, but *Wyrmholes*? —Openings in time and space that attract only Dragons? No humans have ever seen one, but multiple Dragons have!"

"If I am following what you are thinking, are you supposing that they are opened somehow by the species of Dragons we call Wyrms?" asked Lumea.

"I think that is a real possibility," said Tanarul. "But what if they are opened by them from the other side?

No accounts we have heard describe any activity by Wyrms on this side of the Gate."

"So, you're saying that Wyrms on that side are opening the Gate in order to take Dragons from this side into their world?" asked Ayo.

"That is also a possibility," said Tanarul, "but this might also explain, too, what the streaks of light are; the lightning that never strikes the earth but shoots out of sight over the horizon. It's not lightning at all! It's..."

"Wyrms!" exclaimed Lumea. "Wyrms entering our world from theirs and being shot out at such great speed that they ignite in the atmosphere."

"But, being Dragons, they're not burning from the extreme heat," Tanarul continued. "They would have landed many miles away from their entry point."

"And moving at that speed, maybe they could have shot into the earth itself. They could be buried underground," added Viorica.

Everyone nodded at Viorica's suggestion and pondered the situation for a few moments, true to their Dragon nature.

Finally, Lucian cried out, "Vladimir! You told me that no one knows the origins of the Wyrms. Could this be it? Could they have entered our world from another time or another Earth?"

"Science fiction is not my usual form of storytelling," Vladimir replied, "but what Tanarul is saying makes a lot of sense."

"And it's not fiction," said Viorica. "We have talked to witnesses of the event. We have detailed descriptions of the Dragon's Gate event as a reality. Our world Dragon family has lost its own brothers and sisters through it."

"If the Wyrms came through it," said Urk, "wouldn't they have some memory of doing it? Has anyone ever asked one?"

"Until now, I doubt that subject would ever have come up in a conversation," said Viorica.

"Yes, I've never thought to ask, 'Are you from Italy or did you shoot out of a glowing tunnel in time and space?'" said Urk.

"We must interview some Wyrms!" said Tanarul.

"I have a long list of them!" said Lucian. "Maybe I haven't been wasting my time on research after all."

"Research is never a waste of time," said Lumea. "It's the reason for time."

"Great Tanarul?" asked Prunk, "what does a Dragon's Gate look like?"

"Well, as we mentioned earlier, Prunk, it begins as a small patch of light that gradually spins around itself, making larger and larger circles."

"Like that one over there?" Prunk replied, pointing behind the adult Dragons.

Everyone spun around immediately, glancing in the direction Prunk was pointing. Lucian, being human, could not see the circular glowing gate beginning to open, but he knew what was happening from his friends' reactions.

"Don't look at it!" yelled Lumea in a voice louder than Tanarul had ever heard.

"I still feel the attraction!" exclaimed Vladimir. "Fly! Fly away from it!" with his own feet like an eagle, he grabbed the wingless Lumea by the arm and took off into the sky.

Ayo, a spine winged Dragon, took a firm hold on Tanarul's arm and followed.

"Wait! Wait! It's Prunk!" yelled Tanarul. "He's trying to fly after us, but he's too young. He's being pulled into the Gate!"

Ayo made a lightning-fast loop, still holding Tanarul in one arm, and gripped the tail of the floundering Prunk, whisking both of them away to safety.

Fetita was holding on to a tree limb, but the suction of the Gate was too great. The limb broke and she was headed directly into the center of the void. Like Prunk, her young wings could not fly her to safety. Just as she thought it was too late, she felt something latch firmly under her arms. Viorica had grabbed the young Dragon and, with all her power, had flung Fetita straight up into the air, well out of range of the Gate's magnetism.

Viorica, a bat-winged Dragon, had used the free fingers of her wings to rescue Fetita but didn't have time to unfurl her leather flaps and fly herself to safety. She was now far too close to the Gate's irresistible pull. One streak of light shot out of the now-closing gate, and the only sound the other Dragons could hear was Viorica's voice saying, "Oh, noooo!" The gate was closed.

She was gone.

She could not have heard Tanarul's anguished cry of "Viorica!"

Ayo was now descending, still holding Tanarul by the arm and Prunk by the tail. Lumea was also being lowered to the ground by Vladimir, and Fetita had begun flapping her wings from where Viorica had tossed her into the sky. She followed the older Dragons.

Phoebe, being a Phoenix, had felt no pull from the Gate but had been blown safely behind a tree by the strong wind gusts of Vladimir's wings. All of them sadly lined up before the spot where the Dragon's Gate had opened. Tanarul again lowered his head in despair. "Viorica," he whispered.

Ayo suddenly stood at attention. "Where's Urk?" All the Dragons frantically looked around them. Urk was nowhere to be seen.

"Not Urk, too...." moaned Tanarul

Then, from behind a large boulder, a trembling voice said, "He's...he's... with me." It was Lucian.

As soon as the Dragon's Gate had started to open, the brave human had swept Urk into his arms and thrown his body weight on top of the small Dragon, pinning him safely to the ground behind the large rock. Urk now climbed to the top of the bolder, shaking off the dirt and dried leaves. He scanned the surprised but relieved faces of his companions.

"What a ride," said Urk. "Is everyone OK? Wait...where's...

"She's gone," said Tanarul.

9-Land of the Found

Viorica could not stop spinning. She desperately tried to flap her mighty wings into an upright and steady position, but she was unsure where upright was. She seemed to be in an endless tube made of swirling air. The thought of a tornado immediately entered her mind, but the swirling air was not violent but steady, and it seemed to have a substance, even a color.

It could have been made of split pea soup, yet it was not moist. Viorica reached out with the tips of her wings and long fingers to see if she could get a grip on something and discovered the spinning tube was not dry either. She drew her wingtips back quickly because touching the substance just made her spin faster.

Seeing that fighting the situation just seemed to make matters worse, she began to roll herself into a tight ball the way she had seen some human swimmers do as they jumped gracefully into their rivers or pools. Now, in this more relaxed state, she began to recover some sense of where up and down might be.

The spinning tube seemed more like an enclosed roller coaster at this point, but the ride, if it could be called a ride, was now smoother, almost gentle as the split pea soup color of the air started to take on more of a pink tint. Finally, there appeared ahead of her a pinhole of light.

The light grew brighter and brighter, and Viorica felt strongly that she was about to exit the now pinkish wind tunnel. She was one of the fastest and most skillful flyers among the Dragons and prepared to enter the unknown in full flight. She could feel the wind currents begin to spin slower as her sense of gravity started to return.

She took a deep breath, igniting her own internal firebox in case her unknown destination presented some threat. The spinning pink and green air behind her was now reducing into smaller and smaller circles. As the tip of her tail exited the tube, the spinning closed in on its own center, just as the gate had opened back in Romania. Viorica had arrived at her destination.

Her Dragon senses told her she was in no immediate danger as her strong wings took her on a circular flight to survey her surroundings. She saw no reason to let out a blast of fire breath, but she did release a cloud of steam to cloak her presence. It was a hiding method of her own invention, and it required less concentration than chameleon cloaking. She wanted her full attention focused on her new location.

She ascended to have a better look at the landscape in her own cloud of steam. There was not much of interest to see. No vegetation was to be seen, just rocks of all sizes, from pebbles to huge boulders. They seemed ancient, and their jagged edges were rounded by eons of erosion caused by blowing sand. The surface of the land reminded her of pictures human-made explorer robots had taken of the landscape of Mars, which was a planet she was in no hurry to visit.

"Am I on Mars?" she said aloud, even though no living creature was within sight to hear her question.

"Not exactly Mars, but that was a good guess," said a voice above her. Viorica had been so busy studying the landscape that she hadn't noticed the presence of a long, glistening, serpent-like creature above her. It had appeared from behind a pyramid-shaped plateau that reached beyond the low-hanging clouds.

The creature had four legs and a long tail. It was wingless but seemed to gracefully swim through the air just as a water snake glided through a river. The closer it came, Viorica could see its oversized eyes, long flowing mustache, and powerful antlers.

"Chen!" Viorica recognized the legendary Chinese Dragon immediately.

"I am honored to be in the company of the Great Viorica of Romania, inventor of steam cloaking and physician to Dragons of the world," said Chen, "but dismayed to see you in this dismal location."

"I'm sure you know it's not my choice to be here," she replied.

"Nor mine," Chen agreed. "The way of the gate is mysterious. No Dragon can know when its opened door beckons and few can resist the invitation."

"Do you know where we are?" asked Viorica.

"There is one who can answer that question much better than I." Chen answered. "Please join me. She is speaking with the Great Bogdan at this moment."

He quickly air-swam to his right and signaled for Viorica to join him.

Viorica followed him in flight. She was excited by his news. "So, Bogdan is here... and he is unharmed?"

Chen smiled. "I'm sure you know much better than I do that dragons are the most durable beings on the earth, at least on our earth, and are not so easy to harm. We can even exist the hostile atmosphere of this bleak and poisonous place."

As she followed him in flight, Viorica suddenly realized the truth of what Chen was saying. Wherever they were, the temperature was extremely hot, hotter than any human or animal could endure on her home planet. Being a Dragon, she had not been bothered by that fact, nor the smells of toxic gas in the air that would certainly have caused any other earth dweller to drop over in a few seconds. Obviously, only Dragons could survive here.

Their flight led them to the top of the high pyramid plateau. Viorica could see the forms of several Dragons gathered in a circle surrounding a coiled serpent Dragon, the largest Wyrm Viorica had ever seen.

"We are awarded great fortune," whispered Chen as the two of them came to soft and noiseless landings at the back of the Dragon Circle. "The Queen's council has not yet begun."

Viorica and Bogdan locked eyes, and he gestured for her to approach. Though dragons rarely express physical affection, their instincts were elated.

"She is about to speak," Bogdan whispered to Viorica, without questioning why she happened to have appeared amid the gathering. Dragons don't waste a lot of time questioning each other about personal details. Besides, he knew only too well there was only one way to enter this mysterious land. "I've been waiting to hear some answers since Chen, and I first arrived here."

The huge Wyrm had impressive horns that curved in "S" rather like lightning bolts, giving her a regal appearance. Viorica was later to learn that this was Avashai, the Majesta of the Dragons and quite probably the oldest living creature on either of their worlds. On Viorica's world, Avashai would have been called a Queen.

In a commanding volume, but a gentle voice, the Majesta spoke. "I regret to report that I have no additions to the news I shared with you a few hundred years ago," she announced.

There were a few groans from the small gathering for Dragons. Viorica noticed that none of them were serpent dragons. There was a variety of Dragons present, but all with legs, spine-wings, or winged forelegs.

"I can understand your groans and I appreciate your patience since some of you have waited to hear better news for centuries," said Majesta Avashai softly, "but the mystery of the Gate is still unsolved. I know how greatly you must long for the beauty of your own land since I have similar memories of a very different landscape than the one surrounding us now."

Bogdan spoke. "Majesta of all Dragons, though we have never met, I have spoken to many others who are here from my own land, and I understand your sincere desire to return us home safely, and I thank you for that. In my own country, I am called the Leader of the Dragons.

"Yes, I know your name, Great Bogdan," said Avashai "and the title of your office on Earth. Your rule over them must be a great responsibility."

"Dragons rule themselves on my planet," replied Bogdan, "and I provide little more than a place for them to meet."

"If I may interrupt, your Majesta," said Viorica, "Bogdan is far too modest. Our whole species looks to him for guidance and wise advice. No one deserves the title of Leader more."

"A new arrival " said the Queen, "and a loyal subject, I see.

"Viorica is certainly a loyal friend, but not a subject," Bogdan quickly added, "She is the most valuable of team members."

"I believe we have thoroughly covered your admirable system of mutual respect," the Queen continued. "We are pleased to see how progressive our descendants have become on our chosen planet."

"Are you saying we're related to you, Great Majesta?" asked Viorica.

"Allow me to give Viorica a quick history lesson, your Majesty." Bogdan stated.

Chen stood beside them and added, "A wise interjection, Great Bogdan, since the honorable Viorica has been among us less than 10 minutes."

"What are minutes?" asked the Queen.

"Units of human-time measurement of brief periods on our planet, O Majesta," Chen answered, "of little use to one who thinks only in terms of hundreds or millions of years."

The Queen pondered Chen's statement. "Humans, yes, I have heard you speak of them. Bogdan is welcome to take a few million of their minutes for his history lesson."

Bogdan gave a bow of respect to the Queen. "Viorica, coiled on her throne before you, is the Original Dragon, the oldest of our species and grandmother to us all."

Viorica glanced quickly at the huge Wyrm Queen, who smiled and gracefully nodded. The other Dragons in the gathered circle directed their attention to Bogdan:

"Though this is the first time we have officially met Her Majesty, Chen and I have learned of her legend from the other Dragons who entered this realm long before us. It began a few billion of our Earth years ago, when this planet was in the same stages of evolving as our home world.

"First it was a formless void, then on fire with volcanic eruptions and lava flows, all the while sculpting a landscape that would give birth to oceans and land masses. The parallel story continued and finally all species of animal life populated the planet."

"I think I've heard this story before," said a small Dragon who reminded Viorica of Urk.

"No doubt you have," nodded Bogdan. "But, sometime during those eons of early life, Avashai emerged, possessing characteristics of every other species on the planet, except she could breathe fire, fly without wings, make herself invisible, and possess the strength of hundreds of the planet's mightiest creatures. She was the first Dragon- and she was born laying eggs!"

"But, how...? asked the small Dragon.

"Never ask 'how' in the middle of a creation story, my young friend. It's a question no one can answer," Bogdan replied.

Viorica thoughtfully scanned the desolate piles of shattered rocks and dust-filled riverbeds surrounding them. "I'm guessing this planet's history took a dramatic turn from our own."

"You have guessed correctly," Bogdan continued. "As the ages passed, the creatures around Avashai and her family of Wyrms began to change, to take different forms, as reptiles, mammals, and the creatures we call dinosaurs began to populate the growing forests and streams. Majesta's family had not yet begun to grow out of their original state. They seemed virtually immortal compared to the others. What was the hurry?"

"Then it happened." The Queen finally spoke. "The flaming rock, half the size of our moon."

"This planet suffered a similar disaster as our own," Bogdan sighed. "Except on a much greater scale. The giant meteor that struck this version of Earth caused a natural disaster that wiped out every living plant and animal worldwide- forever- except for Dragons, Avashai, and her family."

"I will continue, if I may," suggested the Queen. Bogdan agreed.

The Queen didn't move very quickly. After all, she was countless centuries old. She slowly uncoiled her massive body from her regal pose on the throne and settled into a more comfortable position. She propped her chin on the arch of her tail and began to relate her story:

"My children and I had begun the process of hibernating occasionally, not for long periods of time, but long enough to see that changes could happen during our slumber. They were small changes: longer spine scales, cheek fins, maybe gills for longer swims through the oceans and streams. As Bogdan states, there was no hurry. The animals around us, however, were evolving very quickly since they lived in a predator-and-prey environment. They evolved for their own survival. We took great pleasure in watching them grow and graduate to the next stages from one generation to the next. We were friends to all of them."

"Just as we are back home," said Viorica.

"That is gratifying to hear," said the Queen. "Your outside appearance has changed into a variety of beautiful creatures, but inside you have retained our compassion for those weaker than we are."

"And every Dragon on our Earth evolved from this planet's single species of Wyrms?" asked Viorica.

"Allow me to continue," said Avashai. "After the disaster caused by what Bogdan calls the meteor, a terrible sense of loneliness overcame your ancestors. We no longer lived in a stimulating environment of variety, watching other species evolve and grow. We lost interest in evolving ourselves. Who wants to live in a world that is no longer evolving? All we wanted to do was escape this place."

"So do we!" piped in the small Dragon, whose name was Endurko.

"As well you should!" said the Queen. "Then, one day, a Wyrm named Tirrok discovered that the meteor damage had also damaged our atmosphere, leaving what we were to call 'thin spaces' at various locations around the planet. Tirrok air-swam into the sky with two companions and began to fly in circles to see if he could measure the circumferences of the thin spaces.

In the process, one day his companions saw him suddenly disappear into a circle of his own making and the space-hole close on itself. As he left, they could hear him say, "It's beautiful! Our planet has been restored!"

"He discovered how to open the Dragon's Gate!" Viorica exclaimed.

"As you call it," said the Queen, "Yes, he did, and others followed. Searches for thin spaces continued and soon most of our population had immigrated to the land we thought had been lost to us forever."

"But what does that have to do with the rest of us being vacuumed up into this pile of rocks?" asked Endurko.

"A few hundred years ago, the conditions in our atmosphere changed. We may never know why," said the Queen sadly. "We could no longer travel into your world without Dragons of your home being transported into ours."

"And, when we are here, here we stay," added Bogdan. "The Gate remains closed to us, no matter what we have tried. Only the Wyrms born on this planet can exit through the Gates."

"They have tried to take us with them but have failed every time," said Chen. "Our gracious hosts have opened the Gates many times for us as their young ones were sent to your world. The result of their brave efforts have been even more of your kind being vacuumed into this land of rocks."

"The streaks of light!" exclaimed Viorica. "They really are your young Wyrms being shot like lightning into our better world. Just as we figured."

"As you figured?" asked Bogdan.

"Yes!" answered Viorica. "You must know that after you two disappeared, a team of Dragons would be formed to rescue you!'

"The usual team?" asked Bogdan.

"If by 'usual', you mean Tanarul, Lumea, Ayo, Urk, Lucian, Vladimir, Phoebe, a flock of Hai Riyos, and me -that's the team. Together, we had already connected the Wyrms to the mystery of the Dragon's Gate when I got a little too close for my own good. And here I am!"

"Then, there is hope for all of us!" Bogdan exclaimed. That team has saved our own world several times over. Now it's time to save this one."

10-Digging for Wyrms

Back on planet Earth, Viorica's trusted team was wasting no time. Lucian's research on the origin of Wyrms outlined a clear picture of the current locations of almost every Wyrm in Europe and the surrounding countries. Vladimir and Lumea had prepared a list of questions about information concerning knowledge of the Dragon's Gate legends in the Wyrm branch of the Dragon Family. A flock of two dozen Hai Riyos had been contacted through Berty the Bunyip, and they flowed to Romania from Japan in seven minutes. The flock had already assembled and were waiting for the questionnaires to be completed.

"The oldest of the Wyrms are likely to have more knowledge of their legends," said Tanarul. "Lucian, does your research include their ages?"

"The ages of most of them," Lucian answered, "but it seems to me that the oldest are probably in the Americas. Those will be the hardest to locate. The only reports I have read are suggested by early Canadian and Native American fables. I can't be sure which ones are based on the truth. Nearly all of the Wyrms live in rivers, lakes, and streams, which would also make them harder to find."

"We can't waste time looking for Wyrms that may not even exist!" said Ayo. "Who knows? Viorica's life could be in danger. We need more solid leads."

"Who would know Wyrms better than other Wyrms?" asked Urk. "I'll bet they could wriggle through all this fact-from-fairytale Wyrm hole craziness."

"Urk's right!" said Tanarul.

"I am?" exclaimed Urk. He wasn't used to being right, but the sight of losing Viorica instantly made him think more clearly.

"And you're right, too, Tanarul," said Ayo. "The oldest of them should know the most. Lucian, where is the oldest Wyrm in Europe?'

"Probably this one," replied Lucian, pointing to his screen. His present location is probably in the bend of this remote river in Northern Ireland.

"Ayo and I will fly there now!" declared Tanarul. "The Hai Riyo will cover the rest of the Continent, but since a lot of the Wyrms live underwater, it might take them longer than usual."

"Yeah, maybe eighteen seconds instead of twelve," shrugged Urk.

Fi, the leader of the Hai Riyo flock, joined the conversation. " I'm afraid it will take us much longer than that. We are fliers, not swimmers."

Urk tapped his chin in thought for a moment. "Hmmm, I have a few friends who are. All of us, shall I say, more compact varieties of the family swim like barracudas, but with better attitudes."

"Can you recruit some of your relatives?" asked Tanarul. "One to ride each Hai Riyo?"

"Watch me!" said Urk, darting into the forest. In a matter of minutes, he had returned with a large group of Lesser Dragons who were already getting acquainted with each of their Hai Riyo rides.

"Since I've grown to almost turkey size, the Lessers are showing me a little more respect," observed Urk. He then joined the other smaller Dragons as they planned their strategy. The Hai Riyo would fly. The Lessers would swim.

Urk climbed aboard the back of Shou, his Hai Riyo friend, on an earlier adventure.

"Enough talk," declared Fi. The Hai Riyo and their riders vanished.

"Now that is a team," said Ayo, and turning to Tanarul, asked, "To Ireland?"

Tanarul did not hesitate. He sprang into the air even before Ayo had spread his powerful wings. As he launched, Ayo easily overtook Tanarul and flew over his friend's head, yelling back, "Grab onto my tail, Tanny. You know it's faster." In seconds, they were hidden by the clouds.

Fetita and Prunk watched their friends' quick exit in awe. The two youngest Dragons had not recovered from their shock over the sudden appearance of the Dragon's Gate and the sight of Viorica being vacuumed out of existence.

"It's all my fault," said Fetita. "She saved me instead of saving herself."

"She was so brave," said Prunk, "but now she's...where is she anyway?"

Lumea and Vladimir had just given their list of questions for the Wyrms to the Hai Riyo and their riders. The list was verbal, of course, since Dragons always remember. Now the two elder Dragons approached Prunk and Fetita.

"No doubt the two of you have a few questions," said Lumea kindly.

"And wouldn't it be lovely if we had some answers?" added Vladimir.

"She's gone because of me," said Fetita, through a stream of Dragon tears. "Why didn't she save herself?"

"She didn't because she's Viorica," said Lumea, "and it is her nature to save others. She is the Great Doctor among Dragons. That is what doctors do."

"And you are not to blame for what happened," said Vladimir. "Whenever something happens that nobody can understand, we look around us to quickly decide whose fault it was."

"As if that will explain what we still don't understand." said Lumea.

"Viorica would have done the same for any of us. This time it just happened to be you. Because she's, well, because she's Viorica. The Great Lumea has said it all."

"And now the rest of us will work together to get Viorica as well as our other friends, back among us, because that's who we are," concluded Lumea.

"But what can the two of us do?" asked Prunk.

"Oh, we have special plans for you..." smiled Vladimir.

Before Vladimir could continue, a Hai Riyo appeared. On her back was Huldah the Squirrel Dragon.

"Please excuse us while we hear what Fi and Huldah have to say," said Lumea as he, Vladimir, and the others gathered with Lucian at the cave entrance where the young human sat, tablet in hand.

Prunk watched the older Dragons briefly and then turned to his friend. "Gosh, Fetita! This is really scary! I've never thought about what my part could be. I'm a little nervous. I hope we don't mess up."

"The grownups have been doing things like making important decisions a long time." said Fetita "Whatever they want us to do will be the right thing, but

I think I'm a little nervous, too!"

The two looked at each other as if waiting for the other to say something comforting. Finally, Fetita said "Hey, I remember something Viorica told me once. She said, "being nervous means that you care,"

"Care about what?" Prunk interrupted.

"Care about doing a good job. Stuff like that," said Fetita

Prunk folded his wings to his sides. "Hmmm...they're not going to have us do anything risky, so whatever they tell us to do shouldn't be too scary."

"You're right! They always give us good advice," exclaimed Fetita.

"Especially Viorica!" said Prunk.

"Yes!" said Fetita. "She always knows what is best, and you know what?"

"What?" Prunk replied.

"I know she's gonna come back! I know it! If we don't find a way to save her, she'll save herself. I just know it!"

Prunk finally began to smile. "I know it too, Fetita."

At the cave, Huldah was busy dictating her information to Lucian.

Lucian, Lumea, and Vladimir had not seen Huldah for a few years; since their search for the Dragon Man. She pointed to Lucian's screen as she spoke:

"And then we searched both the Traun and Alm rivers of Austria and you were right Lucian. The Stollenwyrm was taking a snooze in a deep pool in one of the caves. She is not a true Wyrm, of course, with her finned forearms and webbed hands, but is familiar with every known Wyrm in Europe.

She confirmed that Dragon's Gates and Wyrm Holes are one and the same; said it was common knowledge among the Wyrms of her acquaintance, but not one of them had ever said anything else on the subject.

"Did you ask her if she had knowledge about how to open one?" asked Lumea.

"She didn't have a clue," said Huldah, "and seemed surprised that anyone would want to open one since no one knows where they go."

"Did any of the Wyrms remember coming through one?" asked Vladimir.

"They did not." Huldah shook her head. "Their earliest memories are typical of our own infant years; except they had no memories of ever having parents. As they matured, they met other Wyrms who became the only family they knew."

Just as Huldah was finishing her report, several other Hai Riyo transporters appeared, or more accurately, popped into view, being the fastest creatures on the planet. Their excited riders began to speak at once. Vladimir organized them into a line for Lucian to type their information.

"I wish I could type as fast as they can fly," Lucian groaned.

The interviews continued for half an hour, with Shou and Urk reporting last. "I've heard what all of the others have said," Urk commented, "and we might as well have been talking to the same Wyrm. At least they are proving that our theory is right. All of them popped out of those Dragon's Gates as infants and had no idea how to open them again."

Lucian scanned his notes. "Another thing most of them mentioned is that, since the Earth is mostly covered by oceans, the majority of Wyrms must have landed there. That would explain why there are so many sea serpents; Wyrms who have never ventured to the land."

"Finding and interviewing all of the sea serpents could take a thousand years," said Lumea.

"Yes," Lucian replied," and even though that might seem like a weekend to you, I don't have that much time to wait." He continued scrolling through the interviews. "Look at this. Another fact most of the reports have in common is that the oldest Wyrms are in the Americas and that the best resource for locating them is a Wyrm in Northern Ireland! That's where Tanarul and Ayo are headed now!"

"That figures," said Urk. "Those two always have the best adventures."

"But this time we won't have to wait until their return for an update or to see Tanarul's sketches," said Lucian. "Ayo is fully equipped with a new cell phone tucked under his chest scales!"

"Ayo is now shopping online?" asked Urk.

"The phone is courtesy of the Human/Dragon Alliance," Lucian replied. "Sort of a reward for bravery."

"Hmm..." mused Urk. "I wonder if they give a reward for growth. At least that's one I could win."

11-The Oregon Trail

"That must be the bend of the river that Lucian described," said Ayo as he and Tanarul circled for a landing, riding the wind currents created by the winged Dragon's energy.

"Yes, and there's Lake Foyle, where the great Wyrm is supposed to be living, according to Lumea and the St. Patrick legends," said Tanarul.

"What does St. Patrick have to do with it?" asked Ayo.

"I'm sure you've heard the tales of the great Saint banishing all the snakes from Ireland," Tanarul began. "Well, it seems that there was one that Patrick missed somehow. The people of this region call him Lig na Paiste, which means the 'Last Great Reptile'."

"That makes no sense," Ayo observed. "Dragons aren't reptiles.

"When have you ever known a legend to make sense?" laughed Tanarul. "To continue, Paiste, a fearsome river serpent with the horns of a ram, had one day heard of St. Patrick's death. He felt it was once again safe enough to come out to play. He became careless and was often spotted by the residents of the local town near Lake Foyle. Terrified, they begged another holy man, St. Murrough, to perform the same banishing act that Patrick had perfected. He was reluctant, but finally he said OK."

"Obviously, Paiste wasn't banished, or we wouldn't be here," said Ayo.

"Banished enough for the villagers," Tanarul concluded. "He is supposedly being held prisoner at the bottom of this lake and still bound in magical steel rods wrapped around his body. Supposedly, each time he tries to struggle free, the rods become even tighter."

By this time the two of them had landed on the shady banks of the tranquil lake and Tanarul was finishing his story. "And to this day, some of the people from the village swear that the mysterious tides and ripples in the water are caused by old Paiste still trying to cast off those magical steel rods."

"Luckily, they weren't steel," said a voice from the lake behind them.

The ram's horns on a rising creature's huge head glistened in the rays of the setting sun. "They were iron, and they rusted away in no time, at least according to a Dragon's calendar. I'm sure you know I could have melted them away at any time but seeing me struggle in defeat and sinking into the depths did keep the nosey villagers away for a while."

Tanarul and Ayo were elated that they had already found the Dragon of their Irish quest. Ayo urgently began explaining the purpose of their mission in Ireland: the search for the world's oldest Wyrm who they hoped could supply them with vital information about the Dragon's Gate.

Paiste immediately cut short any further reference to his own legend. He became concerned about the whereabouts of the Great Bogdan as well as Chen who were old friends of his. He was troubled the most, however, about the disappearance of Viorica. Her reputation as a healer was well-known to all Dragons.

"The Wyrm you seek is called Wally," said Paiste.

"Wally?" said Ayo and Tanarul in one voice.

"I have not seen him personally for many years, but I am told that Wally is the name he answers to, but don't ask me why. Even in your youth, you must know that Dragons often adopt the pet names humans have given them through the years. Surely you don't think my original name was 'Paiste.' The oldest Wyrm of our species somehow became enamored with the name Wally."

"How can we find him?" asked Tanarul.

Paiste paused to think. "I know of three sources in North America," said the Irish Dragon. "One of them is bound to know his location."

At the Cave of the Dragons, Lucian was still compiling his notes. "A text just came through."

"From Ireland?" asked Lumea.

"From Africa," Lucian replied sadly. "Makeda's great grandmother has died."

Lumea bowed his head. "We become so completely occupied with our own concerns, that we too often forget the troubles of others. What does Makeda's text say?"

"She says that your sister was at her grandmother's side giving great comfort to both of them," said Lucian.

"I knew my sister Sapa would be there," said Lumea. "Gwynn, Makeda's great grandmother had worked with my sister on countless archeological digs since Gwynn was a teenager."

Lucian held on to Lumea's words. The reality of the differences between the life spans of humans compared to Dragons weighed heavily on his heart. Gwynn had been about twice the ages of Prunk and Fetita, who were 50 years old and considered babies among Dragons.

Lumea immediately understood Lucian's expression. "That's why Dragons treasure their friendships with humans above all others. I have learned more about loyalty and friendship from you than I have in several hundred millennia of associations with many Dragons. The length of your years means little compared to the quality of your days among us."

Lucian secretly thought that it would take several lifetimes to fully understand the wisdom of his ancient friend. He blushed at the Great Dragon's compliment. "I suppose being friends with near immortals has made me aware that I should make every day count. I can't make some dumb mistake and then take a hundred years to fix things."

"Lumea smiled. "I've known Dragons whose dumb mistakes could never be fixed, regardless of our 'near immortal' lifespans, as you put it. A correct label. We don't live forever either."

"That reminds me of a question that I've been wanting to ask," said Lucian. "Ever since we've been working together to find Bogdan, everybody has presumed that he is still alive. Then we saw Viorica disappear right in front of us. Why is everyone thinking they've been transported to another realm and not gone forever?"

"Dragons don't immediately think of the worst outcome of any situation, I suppose," Lumea pondered. "In a way, we might appear to people as storybook characters always looking forward to a happy ending. Those storybook characters have the right idea. If we give up at the beginning of problems, the next generation inherits nothing but our failures."

"So, you think the Dragon's Gate mystery will have a happy ending?" asked Lucian.

"I've witnessed a lot more happy endings than sad ones." Lumea replied.

Lucian smiled back at Lumea. Both knew that Lumea seldom answered a question directly. A wise teacher inspires more questions.

"You're making me think on my own again, aren't you?" said Lucian.

"Is that what you think?" asked Lumea in mock surprise.

Urk had stood by silently, which he seldom did, listening to the whole conversation. "This lesson in life could take forever, Lucian, and forever lasts a lot longer for Lumea." By the way, you're getting a message."

Lucian had been distracted from his tablet vigil. "It's from Ayo. He says he and Tanarul have met with their contact in Ireland and are now on their way to search for a Wyrm named Wally."

"Wally Wyrm?" exclaimed Urk. "You and the Great Lumea are discussing the meaning of life and death and they're looking for a cartoon character? Obviously, I should have gone with them."

Lucian shook his head along with Urk, pretending to be frustrated, too, but thinking that "cartoon character" was a pretty good description of Urk, himself.

On the other end of the Wyrm Hole, the small Dragon who reminded Viorica of Urk approached her with a question. "Where were you when you were zapped into this awful place?"

"I was with my friends in Romania," said Viorica. "We had just come back from the Far East where we were trying to figure out this Dragon's Gate problem. Oh, and my name is Viorica. Are you from Romania, too?"

"I am! My name is Endurko, and you don't have to introduce yourself. All Dragons know of the Great

Viorica, world traveler and Healer of All Dragons! Have you come to save us?"

"If I had any idea of how to do that, I certainly would, or at least give it a try," said Viorica sadly.

"Did I hear you say that the Great Tanarul is on the case?" asked Endurko with great enthusiasm. "I heard that he can do anything. He'll get us out of here!"

"According to those stories Vladimir tells, that is true," she answered. "He is a good friend and I have faith in all my friends!"

"Let's go wait for the Gate to open," said the small Dragon.

"You know where it opens?" asked Viorica.

"I know where the Gate to Romania opens. You came through it!"

Viorica had not looked back when she had arrived, so she had no idea where that opening was. Joining the eager young Dragon seemed as good an idea as any other. He was a Swamp-hopper Dragon, who could leap great distances in seconds. She had to fly to keep up with him. Soon they arrived at a rock formation that looked like all of the other piles of rock on the rugged landscape.

"Here we are," said Endurko proudly. "It'll be opening any minute."

"I have no reason to believe otherwise," Viorica agreed. She was telling the truth. She truly did have that much faith in her friends.

Ayo's texts were coming in at a rate of about every half hour. Several of the Dragons as well as Phoebe, the leader of the Phoenix flock, had made a small circle around Lucian as he read them with much excitement.

"Ayo is moving faster than I have ever known him to fly and even with Tanarul as his passenger. He says they're just leaving Ontario and headed for their next stop."

"He really shouldn't text while flying," observed Urk.

"He's not on a freeway," said Vladimir.

"...and well above the flight paths of commercial aircraft," Lumea added.

Lucian chuckled to himself, amused to hear the ancient Dragons speaking so casually about the world of human travel and communications. "You've all become Metro-Dragons! I love it! Look! Ayo also sent the sketch Tanarul had made of the Dragon of Lake Ontario."

"This is Kingstie, the Great Wyrm of Lake Ontario, named by the humans after the city of Kingston," said Lucian.

"Humans are so whimsical, aren't they?" mused Urk.

"Tanarul also reports that the humans have been mistaken in calling her a Wyrm," Lucian continued. "When she emerged from the lake, our friends could see that she had flippers like the Loch Ness Monster."

"Kingstie reported that she had spoken about 40 years ago to Wally, soon after he had adopted that name. She didn't say why he had decided to do that. She said that he was living somewhere in the Northeast United States but wasn't specific. She suggested they could probably learn more on their next stop."

"Where will that be?" asked Vladimir.

"Somewhere in the Catskills mountains, and it will not be to meet another Dragon. They have been given directions to the location of the Great Thunderbird, where he is visiting a nest of his relatives in Upstate New York." said Lucian. "Wait a minute! Thunderbirds are real?"

"As real as a Phoenix," Phoebe answered. "Of course, they are a lot bigger and most of them live in North America."

"I am continually amazed at the world you live in!" said Lucian.

"It's your world, too," said Phoebe, "but most people are too engrossed in their own reflections to believe in it."

"Or too distracted with trivial questions," said Urk. "You're missing another text. Oh, and look at the pretty picture."

"Tanarul's illustration is a good indication that they have already met with the Thunderbird," observed Lumea.

"It's the legend of the Thunderbird's battle with Unidaga, the one-horned Dragon. A legend of a forgotten midwestern tribe, as I recall," said Vladimir. "They were old friends, but battle stories always draw more interest. Tanarul could not resist sketching this during their visit, I see. The story's setting is Granite Peak, the highest mountain in the Beartooth Range of Montana..."

"Get comfortable, everyone. It's story time!" said Urk.

"Sorry," laughed Vladimir. "I was inspired by Tanarul's lovely picture."

"Hmmm... I'm afraid a lovely drawing is all they have to show for that visit," said Lucian. "The Thunderbird gave them a list of over 60 lakes that he's sure Wally visits regularly, and he's confident they will find him in one of them."

"Sixty lakes?" said Urk. "Tell us more about Beartooth Range, Vladimir."

The skies were beginning to turn from bright blue to a sleepy orange on a cloud-scattered evening in the Catskills. Tanarul and Ayo were settling down to sip a few gallons of water on the banks of another peaceful lake like the one they had left in Ireland.

There was a lodge nearby, and they were careful to turn on their chameleon powers to completely disappear from the sight of any hiking humans. They also had the ability to cloak their voices so that their speech would sound like ripples in the lake guided by a gentle breeze.

It was the first time in this search that they had been near any human dwellings. Several hikers from the lodge soon passed by without realizing they were three or four steps in front of two whispering Dragons. One of the women passed to sit down on a timber bench beside the lake, blithely enjoying the beautiful view with her binoculars.

"Over 60 lakes to search!" said Ayo. "Too bad the Hai Riyo are not waterfowl!"

"Oh well, you've been moving super- fast yourself on this trip, Ayo!" said Tanarul.

"It's the least I can do for Viorica!" Ayo replied. "She did save my life once, you know! The first time all of us met inside that secret cave in Kilimanjaro. I've seen her do the same for so many Dragons since then."

"I agree!" said Tanarul. "We'll figure out where Wally is and find out how to save Viorica if we have to search a thousand lakes!"

"Maybe I can help you cut down on that number," said the woman with the binoculars.

Both Dragons froze in place and became silent. How could a human hear their disguised voices?

"And did I hear you say Viorica is in some kind of trouble? Forgive me if I'm not as fluent in Dragon-Speak as you are," she continued, lowering her binoculars. "And don't worry. I can't see you. Only Dragons can detect another cloaked Dragon."

"I believe we are in the presence of Dr. Bunny Campbell, Ayo," said Tanarul with a gentle laugh. "No other person in the United States has mastered Dragon-Speak. And so impressively! Even with our voices cloaked!"

The two Dragons quickly surveyed the area. No other human was to be seen at the moment. The sun was about to drop out of sight. The dragons faded into view, enough to be seen by the now very excited woman but still transparent to anyone a short distance away.

"We are humbled to be in the presence of America's most distinguished Dragonologist, Dr. Campbell. I am Tanarul and this is...'

Dr. Campbell clapped her hands like a 5-year old at a wonderful zoo. "...And this is Ayo, the bravest of Dragons and the perfector of rings of fire! And I certainly know who you are, Tanarul, the cleverest Dragon of them all."

Tanarul sighed, "Vladimir and his social media...and to answer your question, Doctor, yes, Viorica is in trouble."

Neither Tanarul nor Ayo was surprised that Dr. Campbell was also aware of Viorica. Together, they began to hurriedly explain the Dragon's Gate dilemma, the missing Dragons, their information gathering journey, Viorica's heroic rescue of Fetita, her disappearance, and finally their connection to Wyrms, Wyrm holes, and their current search for Wally, the oldest known Wyrm on the planet.

" ...And if that's not enough we are now about to start yet another search somewhere in the Northwest of this country..."said Ayo.

"...diving in over 60 lakes," Tanarul concluded.

"And you think this Dragon named Wally could possibly know how to open the Dragon's Gate?" Dr. Campbell asked.

"That's Tanarul's theory, and he's never wrong!" said Ayo.

"Only in Vladimir's stories, unfortunately," Tanarul added.

Dr. Campbell was silent for a moment as she put her binoculars back in their case. "Unless there is more than one Wyrm named Wally in this country, I think I know where you can find him. And I'll bet you do as well. What is common about the names we humans give your relatives?"

"The most common thread is that they're usually named after the lakes they inhabit or some town very near the lakes," Tanarul reasoned.

"Like Nessie in Loch Ness, or Champ in Lake Champlain, or even Kingstie, who we just met near Kingston," added Ayo.

"We haven't taken the time to memorize the names of every lake and city in this country yet, but we did discuss the possibility of Walla Walla Washington being the place we might find him, but there is no large lake within miles of that City," said Tanarul.

"But, as usual, Tanarul, you're on the right trail," Dr. Campbell smiled, "just to the wrong City and State. "The only legendary lake monster named Wally whom I know about lives in Lake Wallowa, Oregon, near the city with the same name.

"Eureka!" cried Ayo.

"No, Wallowa...as your friend Urk would say," laughed Dr. Campbell.

"You even know about Urk. You truly are the greatest Dragonologist of them all," said Tanarul. "How can we repay you for your information?"

"I have already been paid more than enough by having a real conversation with real Dragons; two of the greatest Dragons of them all!" said Dr. Campbell holding her hands to her cheeks.

"I hope we can come back and visit you when you're back in your home. We've heard of your world- famous collection of Dragon figures," said Tanarul, preparing to spring into the air.

"And maybe next time, uh, Bunny, you would like to take a short ride in the clouds," added Ayo.

The two Dragons then switched off their cloaking and were airborne and out of sight in seconds.

Bunny Campbell was speechless, but inside she was thinking, "Eureka!"

12-One Way Home

The flight to Oregon was a long one from the Catskills. Tanarul had made no attempt to ride Ayo's wind currents. Throughout this entire quest, he had been a passenger holding tightly to the end of Ayo's powerful tail. However, he had filled his lungs with hot air to lessen the load, just as he always did on his solo flights. He knew his winged friend's determination would not have been dampened regardless of the weight he was carrying. Viorica's safety and rescue were his single focus.

"You're an amazing flyer, Ayo," yelled Tanarul as he struggled to hang on, "but, feel free to rest any time!"

"I'll rest after Viorica and all of our friends are safely back in Romania!" said Ayo, in his best superhero voice.

Much to Tanarul's relief, Lake Wallowa finally came into sight through a covering of gray clouds over Oregon. As they descended, the size of the lake became apparent. It would take a lot of diving to determine Wally's location, but Tanarul was ready since his winged companion was not the most graceful of swimmers.

"There doesn't seem to be much human activity on the lake today, thanks to the cloud cover," said Tanarul. "That's something in our favor. Before I start diving, let's discuss a plan. If we can come up with something that might draw Wally out of the lake it would certainly cut down our search time."

"How about some fireworks?" asked Ayo. "There are no humans in sight at the moment."

Without having to use their chameleon camouflage, which drained a lot of their energy, Dragons were able to concentrate on producing more massive streams of fire. As Tanarul counted down. the two of them breathed admirable streams of flames that arched over the length of the lake, rivaling any human fireworks show.

"That should get his attention!" said Ayo, but there was not an extra ripple in the lake. "Let's try again! We'll double the fire!"

Again and again, they tried variations of their signal flares, but still, there was no sign of Wally.

"Our Dragon fireworks show doesn't seem to be working because that's exactly what it would look like from underwater, Ayo. A fireworks show!" said Tanarul. "A human-produced fireworks display would drive Wally deeper into the lake."

"Of course!" Ayo replied. "We're making him think a deserted lake is crawling with humans."

"What he needs to see is a signal known only to Dragons..." pondered Tanarul.

"How about a Dragon's Gate?" asked Ayo.

"You mean..." Tanarul replied.

The idea hit both simultaneously. Both Dragons were young and continually practiced the ancient Dragon art of producing smoke rings as expertly as the masterful elder Dragons. In the process, Ayo had discovered he could also produce even more impressive rings of fire. If he could manage to create a flaming ring big enough, he could simulate the look of the Dragon's Gate they had seen in Romania.

"Stand back!" declared Ayo. "This is for Viorica!" He began to pace back and forth, taking deep breaths, deeper and deeper until he filled his lungs with more fuel-burning oxygen than he had ever inhaled. As he held his breath, the fire box in his throat ignited, awaiting the flap of his closed throat to open for the supply of oxygen to flow. He leaned over backward, bracing for the blast with his wings propped firmly against the rocky shore.

Tanarul had been surveying the cloud cover, waiting for the darkest of them to supply the proper background for an impressive display. "Now!" he yelled.

Ayo's blast of fire was the greatest of his young life. The ring of fire he produced was exactly the circumference of the Romanian Dragon's Gate. He even managed to make it circle itself multiple times, increasing the illusion. The display lasted for several seconds before dissipating into the low-hanging clouds. Ayo's wings relaxed and he fell back on the shore, drained and exhausted.

"Look, Ayo!" exclaimed Tanarul. "Under that lonesome pine!"

A tall pine tree grew alone near the tip of one of the lake's many jutting peninsulas. From the water at its end, a horned head slowly began to ascend with its nose fixed on the location where Ayo's fire rings had just lit up the sky.

The creature immediately sensed the presence of other Dragons, and glanced to his right where Tanarul was helping Ayo to his feet. "The last time I saw one of those, a wooly mammoth blundered by and blocked my view." Wally commented. "How did the two of you resist its attraction?'

"Because it was not an actual Dragon's Gate, Great Wally," said Tanarul. "It was a simulation created by my friend here."

"Impressive," said Wally. "Your friend is extremely gifted to have fooled The Gate's creator. And you also know my name, although, on my home planet I was known as Tirrok."

"But you prefer the name Wally now, we are told," said Tanarul

"Yes, it's so much friendlier than Tirrok, don't you think? Why did the two of you summon me? It must be an important reason for you to have gone to so much trouble."

"I'm glad you asked," Ayo said. "Here's our story..."

The two Dragons once again recited the same events and challenges surrounding the Dragon's Gate mystery and the reason, they had decided to seek out the oldest Dragon of the Wyrm Species. Wally listened with great interest.

"And you have already told us that you were the first of your species to open up the Gate, so our question is: can you open it again and release our friends from the other side?"

"I'm sure I could give that a try if it were possible for me to open it. However, as soon as I arrived on this beautiful planet, I was aware that there was an ability I lacked here that is essential to opening the Gate," said Wally.

"What ability is that?" asked Ayo.

"Flight!" Wally answered. The Wyrms on my home planet have the power of wingless flight like many of the Dragons in Earth's Asian nations. Here, we are earth-bound, or more often, water-bound since many of us prefer the feeling of flight as we swim through the water."

"Are you the only Wyrm on Earth who, at least, would know how to open the Gate if you could become airborne?"

"Likely, yes," Wally reasoned. "After I discovered how the Gate or Wyrm Hole opened, others followed, but they used it to rescue their newly hatched children from their planet's hostile environment. The rest of the Wyrms now living on Planet Earth have no memory of ever being on another planet."

"That explains why all of the Wyrms we interviewed don't know any more about the Gate than we do," said Tanarul.

"If we could get you into the sky, do you think you could open it again?" asked Ayo.

"Hmmm," said Wally," but it would take more than one Dragon to carry me since I have to fly in the pattern of a perfect circle."

"How about a hundred or more very small, but very strong flying Dragons?" asked Ayo.

"Do you know that many?" asked Wally.

"Many more than that," said Tanarul. "Would you be willing to come with us to Romania?"

"Since I'm the one who started all of this mess, that will be my pleasure. We must try to get your friends back at all costs," said Wally.

"Why do you suppose the Gate vacuums up Dragons of other species in the first place?" asked Tanarul.

"How can any of us know?" Wally asked. "Maybe some sort of magnetic energy that attracts only Dragons, or some magical balance of nature law that replaces one species for another. I didn't create the effect. I just learned how to use it."

"Did the Gate always take in Dragons from this side when Wyrms from your world passed through it?" asked Ayo.

"I was not aware that it ever did until I started hearing the Dragon's Gate stories." Wally continued. "We do shoot out of it like flashes of lightning; not a good time to be taking note of what's happening around us."

"I'm sure Lumea and Vladimir can come up with exactly why it happens after a thousand- year study, Tanarul," said Ayo to his friend. "Meanwhile let's get Wally to Romania and see if we can get that Gate open!"

"Some Hi Riyo assistance would be a good idea," said Tanarul.

Ayo immediately reached for his prized cell phone. Thirty-seven seconds later, ten Hai Riyo were fitting

Wally with comfortable carrying straps and mapping out a flight pattern to Romania. Ayo was texting an update to Lucian about their success so far, and that he and Tanarul would be flying back on their own.

Back in Romania, before Lucian had finished reading Ayo's text, the Hai Riyo had arrived carrying their precious cargo.

"Welcome to Romania, Wally of Wallowa!" Lumea declared. "I am Lumea Veche. We are grateful for your generous willingness to help!"

"Even in the depths of the greatest of lakes, the name Lumea Veche is known and honored," said Wally with a slight bow of his head as he slithered out of the Hai Riyo's harness.

"They'll continue complimenting each other for a while," said Urk to Lucian. "What else does Ayo's text say?"

"He says Wally is willing to try to open the Gate, but he will need some assistance. His species no longer has the gift of flight on this side of the Wyrm Hole and..."

"Say no more," said Urk. "I know exactly who can help him. A squadron of Flitter Dragons just flew in from Greenland and volunteered to help in any way they can. They are about the size of falcons, very strong, and experts at flying in formation."

"Do you think they can carry Wally? He's pretty big." said Lucian.

"Look at him. He has handles!" said Urk.

Lucian glanced at Wally and noticed that instead of having spine fins, he had two sets of side fins running the length of his long body. "I see what you mean!"

Urk immediately headed for the Carpathian cave where the Flitter Dragons were camping and soon returned followed by a cloud of them flying in a huge

formation that looked like a British Harrier jet.

"Typical friends of Urk," Lucian thought aloud.

Introductions were made. Lumea and Vladimir thanked Urk for his quick thinking. Soon, the Flitter Dragons and Wally were taking practice flights to perfect the correct circumference and speed that would create the Dragon's Gate opening.

Other Dragons had continued to gather at the cave to help and witness the event. Thalia the Tatzlewyrm, with her distinctive feline features, stood out in a continually growing crowd of Dragons of all sizes and shapes.

"I came as soon as I heard of Viorica's disappearance! We must save her! I thought Dragon's Gates were exclusive of the Far East, not right here at home in Romania," said Thalia, nervously licking her paws and stroking back her whiskers.

Wally had scouted the area in search of the exact location of the thin place in the atmosphere where the first Dragon's Gate had opened. "There are not a lot of these thin spots around the planet. To my knowledge, they are in China, Australia, New Zealand, Hawaii, here in Romania, and some sort of Dragon retreat area they call Shangri-La."

"We have contacted eyewitnesses in every area you mentioned, "Lumea said. "They can provide some general directions."

"That's all I'll need," Wally replied. "The magnetism of the thin place itself will draw me to the exact spot, just as it did here. If the Flitter Dragons are ready, I am. Shall we try this?"

After several test flights, it was concluded that a precise formation of 126 Flitter Dragons would be required to fly Wally in the ideal pattern that would unlock the Gate. Additionally, approximately 50 dragons of varying sizes had gathered around to observe the trial run.

"Wait for us!" yelled a voice from the sky. Ayo and Tanarul were descending through the thick Romanian cloud cover. They had made it home in record time from far-away Oregon. They took their place in the crowd between Thalia and Urk. Several of the other Dragons pulled cell phones from under their chest scales to record the historic event.

"Metro-Dragons..." Lucian smiled and thought to himself.

Wally gave his flight crew the signal and was gracefully lifted above the ground. As they began the spinning process, their circle gradually shifted from a horizontal spin to a vertical one.

"Perfect!" said Wally, as their spin rate increased for several seconds at a steady pace. About two minutes into the spin a dim light started to make the circular path a little brighter. As tension mounted, the glow became more intense. Then, suddenly threw out a few sparks that made electrical popping noises and the glow was completely extinguished. Wally gave the signal to return to the ground.

"Something isn't right," said Wally. "That is exactly how the Gate was opened on the other side."

"Maybe the temperature is too cold here and the air is too damp under the cloud cover," observed Vladimir.

"That's a good possibility!" said Wally. "The temperature on my planet is much hotter than here -too hot for any human or any other animal, besides Dragons, to survive."

"Lucian!" said Lumea. "Please take shelter in the deepest part of the cave. Phoebe! Please take your flock and warn all of the animal life in the immediate area to hide themselves deep in the thick woods."

"We'll help!" said Urk as he and dozens of the smaller Dragons joined Phoebe and her flock.

"Yes! We must work together to give Wally the right conditions," said Thalia.

Each of the Dragons knew exactly what to do to make the area safe for all their non-Dragon neighbors.

After half an hour had passed, Phoebe gave the all-clear signal. All the non-Dragon animals were now a safe distance away. Lucian was tucked behind some thick stalagmites in the deepest passage of Bogdan's cave.

Again, Wally signaled the Flitter Dragons and soon they were in position as before.

"Ready...Now!" yelled Vladimir.

Every Dragon in the large crowd pointed their snouts straight up beneath the spinning circle and released steady streams of scorching Dragon fire high into the sky, surrounding the spinning circle and instantly changing the atmosphere from moderate to oppressive.

"PERFECT!" yelled Wally. The glow around him began to increase in brightness, by the second, to its maximum intensity.

"It's working!" exclaimed Ayo, between blasts of his own flaming breath. But, nothing happened! The fire-breath and spinning were steady. The circle's glow remained steady. No sparks flew, no opening appeared within the circle, no Dragons were returning from the other world.

"STOP!" yelled Wally.

Back on the ground, the air began to cool again. As the Dragons were catching their breaths, Wally raised his weary head and spoke. "I can't understand it. You made the atmosphere exactly like the one back home and the glow of the opening gate looked and felt just as it should. Thanks to the Flitter Dragons, I circled the thin space exactly as I did back home. What was the problem?"

No Dragon had an answer. Everyone had seen the bright glow, but the gate remained closed. Finally, Tanarul, deep in thought, quickly snapped his head high and tightly clasped his hands together. "That's the problem!"

"What's the problem?" asked Wally.

"You made the circle to open the Gate exactly as you had done it back home. You flew in a clockwise circle! On this side of the gate, the circle to open it would be counterclockwise! A clockwise circle would close the gate, not open it!"

"Genius, as usual," smiled Lumea.

All the other Dragons were nodding in agreement.

"Shall we test Tanarul's theory?" asked Wally.

Not one Dragon, not even Urk, uttered a word. They began inhaling deep breaths of the refreshed oxygen to produce even stronger flames than before. The Flitter Dragons again carefully lifted Wally back into the same position for the rotation to begin. Their leader, who was standing on Wally's head, gave the command," Flip positions... NOW."

Without losing their grip on Wally's side fins, the little flyers in unison flipped to face the opposite direction. They now slowly began their counterclockwise rotation of the Great Wyrm's body. As they achieved their optimum rotating speed, Tanarul yelled, "Ignite!"

The atmosphere's heat again became unbearable for all but Dragons. The glow around Wally was brighter than ever. For three or four long seconds, nothing else changed. Then, within the glow, a blue gray hollowness began to appear. The swirling colors within it started rotating quickly.

A small spinning shape faded into its center. The shape grew larger and began tumbling out of the rotating colors, landing with a thud into the winged arms of Urk, knocking the small Dragon backward.

"Cousin Durk!" exclaimed the surprised little Dragon, flapping his wings to regain his footing. His cousin, known to Viorica as Endurko, had been missing for decades. Both of them quickly turned to look once again toward the still very active Dragon's Gate.

Another shape had appeared, this one longer and more graceful than the tumbling Durk. It was Chen, the sky swimming Dragon who had no problem navigating his way through a storm. He burst forth and began flying around the circle of Dragons on the ground as another shape appeared in the swirling Gate.

"Allow me to introduce to you our Leader, the Great Bogdan, Dragon of Romania!" Chen formally announced.

Bogdan emerged with his wings locked in a sailing position and flew in a vertical loop high above the crowd, obviously elated to be free in his own land again. Several of the fifty Dragons could nor resist cutting off their flames and cheering for their returned leader. As they cheered, the temperature started dropping and the glow of Wally's circle began to flicker.

"Not now!" yelled Tanarul. "Flames now! Cheers later!"

The crowd of Dragons immediately understood, as the Dragon's Gate had already started to collapse, and there was not yet any sign of Viorica. The anxiety of the crowd began to rise. Both Chen and Bogdan realized the situation and began contributing their own powerful flames to the scorching atmosphere. The flickering decreased slightly until an unexpected burst of flames shot out of the middle of the Gate itself.

Suddenly, the glow was completely restored as the familiar form of Viorica casually and gracefully flapped her way out of the void. With her own blazing breath making the Gate's glowing circle brighter than ever before, Viorica had helped save herself.

This time, no Dragon in the crowd could resist cheering. The atmosphere immediately began to cool down and the exhausted Flitter Dragons gently lowered their heroic passenger back to the ground. Viorica was already beginning to embrace her friends, saving Tanarul for the longest hug. "I knew you would figure out a way to bring us back!" she said, with much joy as well as pride.

"Oh sure," said a rather embarrassed Tanarul, "me plus a couple hundred other Dragons, plus some very wise human advice."

By now, Lucian was carefully emerging from his cave sanctuary, staying clear of the entrance rocks that were still too hot to the touch. Viorica swept him up in her winged arms and said, "Yes, humans do have their uses."

She nearly dropped him however, as two small Dragons had flown full force to wrap themselves around her long neck. Prunk and Fetita had been hidden behind the large gathering of adult Dragons the entire time, contributing their own flames to the effort.

"We had to take part in saving you, Great Viorica!" said Fetita, "since saving me is what took you away from us, but I knew you'd come back!"

"We just knew it!" added Prunk.

"And your faith brought me back," said Viorica. "We're even."

"Yes, you both have done your jobs well," said Vladimir, who had finally made it through the crowd of cheering Dragons.

"Our Jobs?" asked Prunk. "But you never told us what our jobs were."

"We didn't have to tell you," said Vladimir. "Your jobs were to be children, and nobody does that better than you. We needed team members who just knew in their hearts that we'd get our friends back. And we did. You were our experts!"

Epilogue

Several months had passed since the mystery of the Dragon's Gate had been solved, but the company of Dragons had been busy transporting Wally to each of the thin places around the world. In Hawaii, Kapulei and Kihawahine had been reunited with their friends. Kari was thrilled to finally have her family back together in New Zealand after her brothers had joyfully popped out of the glowing Gate. Another reunion followed in Australia and another in Shangri-La, where the Dragons, who had been eager to see what was behind the Gate, had learned that paradise is really a beautiful place in their own minds.

Many Dragons, including the Flitter Dragons and many fire-breathers, made up the International Dragon Rescue team since they had to duplicate the atmospheric conditions they had perfected in Romania. The operation also included the rescue of the few remaining Wyrms from the other world, which Viorica finally named Netherplace.

The last Wyrm immigrant to leave Netherplace was the first of the Dragons, Avishai, the Magesta herself. A huge celebration in her honor greeted her through the Romanian Gate. Her exit from Netherplace left it an empty planet. The Dragon's Gates would never be opened again, and the danger was over.

Viorica had volunteered to lead the rescue teams, and even took Fetita and Prunk along on two of the trips. They were elated and very proud to be part of anything involving Viorica. Bogdan had proposed that the highly respected Viorica be appointed the next Leader of the Dragons. Bogdan, who had gained fame as the model for the Seal of Dracula, declared that it was time for a leader who was qualified, not just popular.

Lumea had commented that there had never been a better Leader than the humble Bogdan, a Dragon who always listened to the advice of others and never let his own ego cloud his decisions.

Lumea and Vladimir, assisted by Phoebe and countless smaller Dragons, had decided to stay home instead of joining the traveling team. They had begun an important research project. "Since opening a Dragon's Gate to a highly unpleasant world such as Netherplace is possible, imagine the possibilities of visiting better ones!" Lumea had declared.

Urk and Durk were making up for several hundred years of lost time, sharing outrageous stories of the adventures each of them had experienced while they were apart. "I still can't believe how much you have grown!" said Durk. "You're enormous, even taller than a goose or even a turkey!" Since Durk was about the size of a chicken, it was easy to understand his wonder.

"I would never have grown to this great height if I hadn't saved the magical Golden Gryphon from the carnivorous ice rabbits," said Urk. "Oh, tell me about it!" said Durk, hopping as only a Swamp Hopper can hop.

"Surely he can't believe Urk's stories are true," said Ayo.

"What does it matter as long as they're good stories?" Tanarul answered.

Ayo had to agree. He and Tanarul were just returning from Africa, where they had flown Lucian for an extended visit with Makeda, who had decided to carry on in her great-grandmother's place as Sapa's archaeological partner. Lumea's sister was thrilled to continue their work together as a family.

Ayo and Tanarul had also made good their promise to return for a visit with Dr. Campbell to see her legendary Dragon figure collection and give her that once-in-a-lifetime ride through the clouds.

"Well, Tanny, things seem to be pretty quiet around the old cave," said Ayo. "No more mysteries to solve since the 'Counter-clockwise Solution.' I never asked why you were always so interested in the direction of the Gate's spin?"

"Oh that," Tanarul answered. "At first, I wanted to make sure it was not some kind of natural event, like a tornado. They usually spin counterclockwise above the Equator and clockwise below. When we discovered that the Gate's opening spun the same way above and below, I ruled out any act of nature."

"And that reminded you to ask Wally about the direction he was spinning? Brilliant!" said Ayo.

"Ha! -Just a little extra attention to detail, Ayo," said Tanarul.

"You'll be brilliant when Vladimir tells the story. Get used to it." Ayo replied.

"Vladimir does love his adventure tales," sighed Tanarul.

"I could use another adventure," said Ayo. "I suppose I should fly back to Kilimanjaro now. Maybe there's a monkey caught in a tangled vine back home who needs saving."

"Every day doesn't have to be an adventure, Ayo," said Tanarul. "Maybe there's a game on Lucian's old laptop we could play."

Ayo, usually the bravest of all Dragons, shuddered at the thought.

At that moment, Bogdan was checking out the old laptop himself. "Tanarul! Ayo! I may have something here that will interest you. It's a text from Bertie the Bunyip in Australia. He says that he has a situation there and could use some assistance. He also asks if the two of you are available."

"A situation?" asked Ayo. "What kind of situation?

"What does it matter, Ayo? We were about to play one of those games with Dragons as evil monsters!" exclaimed Tanarul.

"Tell him we're on our way!" declared Ayo, assuming yet another fists-on-hips super-hero pose.

A few seconds later, the two friends were airborne and headed southeast.

Lumea and Vladimir looked to the sky.

"Off to find another adventure, I suppose?" asked Vladimir.

Lumea smiled. "The adventures seem to find them!"

Lumea watched his eager young friends as their silhouettes grew smaller in the sky. He blew a smoke ring that surrounded their image.